CW00552801

BLACK VEIL

GREG JOLLEY

Black Veil

Copyright © 2020 Greg Jolley

All rights reserved. No part of this publication may be reproduced,
distributed, or transmitted in any form or by any means, including
photocopying, recording, or other electronic or mechanical methods,
without the prior written permission of the publisher, except in the case of
brief quotations embodied in critical reviews and certain other
noncommercial uses permitted by copyright law. For permission requests,
please write to the publisher.

This book is a work of fiction. The characters, incidents, and dialogue are
drawn from the author's imagination and are not to be construed as real. Any
resemblance to actual events or person, living or dead, is entirely
coincidental.

Published by Épouvantail Books, LLC.

ISBN 9781087885469 (Hardcover)

ISBN 9781087885476 (Ebook)

For information, write:

Épouvantail Books, LLC

https://epouvantailbooks.godaddysites.com

Cover design: Fay Lane

Dedicated to
The brilliant and inspired film director, Justin R. Diemert

In memory of all the members of the Donner Party.

"When normal life goes into eclipse"

~ Robert K. Ressler

CHAPTER 1

Film Title: Rascals – The Sequel
Production Day: One
Story Date: April 16, 1846

*T*he first explosion inside the munitions warehouse launched timbers, hot shards of metal, and body parts out across the wharf. Black plumes of hot smoke boiled upward, clawing from the windows as the roof blew apart, feeding a downdraft of cruel oxygen to the angry orange flames. Yellow bursts of ammunition cooked off. Rounds of steel-balled cartridges fired in all directions. Reverberations from the secondary blasts of the crates of dynamite blanked out the screams and cries, which went on, anyway, from those still living and *erasing* those of the dying. Out on the wharf, distraught, stunned, and wounded dock workers dove behind wagons and shipping pallets as others were torn apart by flying, burning debris.

Eleven-year-old Sarah Graves appeared from the side of

the brick warehouse under a rainstorm of flaming wood and metal shrapnel. Her face, hands, and arms were blackened, her path changing as she climbed, dove, and ran through the crashing beams of timber and sections of falling brickwork. Right on her heels, a vengeful open mouth of flames opened, its teeth of wood and stone chomping.

Her sister, six-year-old Frau Graves, leaned out of a third-story window followed by a launched coil of rope. The hair on the right side of her head was smoldering, her face was scraped and pale and bleeding from wounds to her ears and nose. Climbing out, she clenched the coarse horsehair line with her little hands, her smock and coat pocked by smoking burn holes and flaming embers. The girl's eyes were tightened down with fearful resolve belied by the beginning of a beautiful, satisfied grin.

The cast iron fire bell clanged from further up the wharf from the cobblestone plaza where child workers squatted, kneeled, and lay, staring open-mouthed into the devastation in the southwest corner of the shipyard waterline.

Three of the young workers staggered onto the loading dock, their clothing in flames, their cries piercing the echoes from the blasts. One was cut to his knees by the bloody punch of bullets exploding out through his chest like a high-speed pitchfork. A deafening secondary blast inside the building propelled a heavy work table out through the doors, decapitating the second and propelling his headless body out onto the cobblestones, where it slid to a crash against a lorry parked across the way. The third worker was missed by the table but was cut vertically in two as a sheet of hammered metal was flung from the building like an errant, deadly toy.

Sarah and Frau Graves met up, eye to eye, kneeling on the stones as brick and wood continued raining down, their heads temporarily sheltered by the burning tool wagon they were under. Their eyes were locked on each other—the older girl appearing stunned in disbelief, the younger one no longer grinning. Frau Graves took her sister's hand, looking wide-eyed for a path through the burning, twisted carnage. Helping her up, she led the way.

Reaching the edge of the warehouse yard where the wharf boards replaced the stone road, they ran as best they could while still hunched forward. Shrapnel was still flying and impaling anything in its path as additional explosions tore through the warehouse.

A secondary explosion of chemical and powder stores eviscerated the interior of the first floor of the building, adding coils of thick black smoke under launched beams and timbers.

The town bell continued its deep and dulled ringing from the tower in the vendor square. Two platoons of well-armed, diminutive child–soldiers double-stepped from the harbor garrison, in effect cornering the chaos. Their rifles poised to fire, they turned every which way, eyes frightened and deadly. Fire wagons rolled up before the warehouse, staying well back of the flames and continuing explosions, the crews making no moves to unfurl the hoses or work the pumps.

Running along the wharf boards right at the edge of the foul and stagnant harbor, Sarah and Frau Graves breathed the eye-burning stench of human and farm waste, the oily water mottled with village refuge.

"This one," Frau Graves yelled, pointing with her small, filthy hand to the stern of the fishing trawler named *Desperation*.

Both staggered as their boots snagged in a nest of fishing nets abandoned on the planks. Frau Graves led her sister along the boards past a sail-powered cargo vessel, weaving around crates and hoisting arms and a small flock of sheep. Wild-eyed young sailors were bent low, staring at the boiling black smoke climbing over the wharf.

Passing along the sail ship's starboard side, its mast was smashed by a flying strongbox wagon of exploding dynamite, slaughtering and torching crew members. They ran to the gangway of the long boat to their right, a worn and run-down fishing craft. The plank ramp to the *Desperation* was guarded by a squatting, jaw-dropped boy. His unbelieving eyes were sweeping from the fire on the ship beside them and across the black water to the burning warehouse. He had dropped his flintlock to his feet where it lay forgotten.

Sarah Graves brushed past him, knocking him aside. Frau Graves shoved even harder, shouting, "There, there, now. Few fireworks is all."

The disheveled and filthy-clothed crew were huddled low on the foredeck, ducking and scampering along the port rail for stolen views of the carnage on the wharf and the burning ship ten yards away. Sarah and Frau Graves jumped from the gangplank and tumbled to the deck, landing before the decapitated head of a goat. Its blood-soaked body lay a few feet away, a twitching, kicking mess. Sarah Graves booted the head away while Frau Graves studied the crew of children.

"Lord, they're an ugly lot," she piped, looking at their young faces and bodies. Without exception, each was badly maimed and injured.

"Who the rip are you?" a kneeling, angry-eyed sailor yelled at them.

"Stroke the boilers!" another youth hollered.

Before the sisters could answer, an explosion on the opposite ship launched a steel axle joint across the dock. A young girl's back exploded in crimson as the hot orange shrapnel tore through her chest. The impact launched her into the side of Sarah and Frau Graves, bowling both over.

"Get us out of here!" Frau Graves yelled at the huddled sailors.

4

"We're short crewed!" a frightened boy called back. He was crouched against a sail-wrapped beam, pulling inch-long slivers from his neck and shoulder.

"The captain's ashore!" another yelled, waving at the oily smoke rising from the embers on the deck.

"Skipper's at the pay house!" another frightened voice called.

"We'll go nowhere without pay," a tall, angry-eyed boy barked.

A volley of musket fire tore through the din. The head of a young sailor disappeared with a cascade of bloody spray. Her body remained upright, her hands and arms still stroking the smoke for fresh air before her missing head. Seconds passed before her bones and muscles gave up the ghost and she crumbled to the deck.

"They're firing at *us*!" a disbelieving voice cried, the sailor on her haunches in between the rail and casks.

"Not us. *Them*!" The tall boy pointed at the sisters, flinching and dropping as the muskets discharged again.

Bullets dug into the wood and sparked off metal as the second round struck the foredeck.

"Who are you?" yelled a short, overweight sailor on his hands and knees.

"No time for that!" another called up from the main deck.

"Lines in!" he shouted the command.

At the fore and aft rails, child sailors swung axes at the cleated ties rather than work the knots. With three deft stokes, the ship was freed from the dock.

"We need full steam. And now!" Sarah Graves bellowed, clambering to her feet and running to mid-deck for the ship's wheel.

"Stroking the boilers!" a crew member screamed up through the deck hatch.

The sailors on the foredeck ran for their stations, leaving

Frau Graves kneeling on the blood-soaked boards in the fire and smoke, destroyed casks and crates, and the two dead bodies. Pushing the severed sheep head aside, her tiny blackened hands tore into the pockets of the dead bodies, pulling out a few coins from each. Pressing them deep inside her sock and left boot, she crawled away.

The approaching soldiers fired another salvo. The long boat was backing into the harbor, bullets sending up sprays of wood. A youth cried out in dying disbelief. A plume of hot, sparking smoke billowed from the steel exhaust spout at the back of the helm where Sarah Graves was cranking the large, spoked wheel as fast as her thin arms could swing.

The bow turned, the trawler listed, and the props spun in the filthy black water. The platoon of blue-coated Spanish soldiers lined up on the wharf, their lieutenant commanding another volley with a down sweep of his saber.

"Get down!"

"Look out!"

"Find cover!"

Bullets struck like deadly knives of steel. Chunks of railing flew and deadly wood shards were launched. A high-pitched scream of pain came from somewhere in the chaos. The boat was ten yards off the dock, leaning hard to starboard as its engines spun at full throttle, propelling the fishing craft out and away.

A sailor crawled to the side of Sarah Graves and stood up.

"Name's Trenton, why are they after you?"

"I might've been the one who dropped the match," she swept smoke from her lovely face and coughed.

"It's not going to stop the slaving, but it was an impressive explosion."

"Thanks," she spun the wheel fast in the opposite direction. "I need more steam!"

Trenton bashed the throttle bar forward, setting off signal

bells. The long boat shuddered and wood beams and metal groaned. He stared at her, beautiful even in her dirty and torn and ember-smoldering dress and coat.

The long boat responded painfully to the change in pace and the turn but gathered speed away from the wharf and out into the low-tide harbor of Puerto Mita. Looking away from her, Trenton stared out across the waters.

"The rocks!" he shouted. "The tide's too low!"

Sarah Graves looked forward and grimaced. The waters to the open sea wove between encrusted boulders and dangerous rocks.

"We can make it!" she yelled back, trying to see how.

From the right side of the harbor mouth, cannons fired with white puffs of smoke. Along the ramparts of the Spanish fort came the deep thundering booms. Seconds later, the overhead rigging came crashing down from the foremast and yardarm, smashing onto the main deck. A fountain of ugly black water rose twenty yards forward of the bow, the second cannonball missing the trawler.

The planks underfoot shuddered as the vessel took a waterline hit from the next roar of cannon fire. Crew members dove for cover as the deck leaned hard to port. Sarah Graves was still on her feet, spinning the wheel. Squinting into the dense smoke, she studied the passage, ignoring the cannons, looking for a way to snake to open water.

"We'll never make it!" Trenton climbed to his feet. "You're going to get us all killed!"

"Not today!" she yelled back.

Frau Graves climbed through the broken mast timbers and furled and burning canvas, clawing her way to the forward hatch. Swinging her small legs out into the darkness below, her hands gripped the stair rails and she lowered herself into the heat and chaos of the engine room. Flames were licking the joist and beams as the boilers and engines screamed in a metallic roar. The cracking of timbers mixed with panicked shouts and cries of agony.

Seeing that one of the boilers was unmanned, she struggled to it. Taking up a shovel, she went to work feeding the open mouth of flames. The long boat made an aggressive turn to port. Behind her, a sailor screamed, toppling into the open box of the transmission. His body was half-consumed in the grinding gears. He was still screaming and spraying blood when the top half of his body crunched and disappeared.

A one-legged coaler shoved Frau Graves hard, knocking her aside as he planted his good foot in the mountain of coal.

"The breach!" he shouted at her, tearing the shovel from her hands.

Making her way forward around the engines, she splashed through two feet of water to the chubby boy struggling with hammer and wedges trying to stem the spraying seawater. At his heels were wooden buckets of saws and shims and a box of square-head nails and rail spikes. Pulling a horse-hair brush from a cask of tar patch, she slathered the first seam he pounded a board over.

"Make it fast! When we level, we'll be swamped." He turned his half-burned face to her, his eyes narrowed, steeling himself from panic.

A sailor reversed the bilge while another pumped the hand bar. A third youth turned the hose to the flaming beams. Frau Graves and the rotund boy were blasted as the nozzle swept around to the fire. Both were knocked from their feet, their filthy clothing drenched. Under the smoke boiling from the low ceiling, embers circled, orange gnats sizzled as they landed in hair and headscarves. The goats penned in the forward steerage were thrashing and braying.

Frau Graves got to her feet and took up a mallet.

Pounding nails into a second board, she was splattered with black pitch as the overweight boy at her side splashed and sealed the seams.

"Should hold," he shouted, stumbling back from the repairs.

"Let's hope," she yelled back and crawled through the tight space between the two steam engines to the left side transmission where what was left of the dead sailor lay under the housing. Kneeling before the gore and shredded clothing, she dug in with her hands. Finding a bit of fabric with a pocket still attached, she pilfered a few farthings and stashed them inside her sock and boot.

"God will smite you!" the round sailor with the melted face shouted at her.

"He's gonna have to get in line," she yelled back.

A one-armed sailor stumbled down the hatch steps, sweeping away smoke from her eyes.

"You! You're wanted topside!" she yelled at Frau Graves.

Climbing to her feet, Frau Graves squeezed between the boilers and shoved past her, heading for the top deck.

The long boat was struggling but running fast, its port side rail low over the water. The starboard side of the hull struck a crag, timber cracked, and the boat shuddered, knocking most of the crew to their knees.

A third round of cannon fire boomed from the northern wall of the fort. This one sent maniacal twirling chain shot. One tore into the water, sending up a fountain in their wake. The other decapitated the flag struts above the stern rail. At the helm, Sarah Graves spun the wheel, the boat still at full throttle. With the final rock outcropping cleared and the bowsprit aimed at the swells washing the harbor exit, she gripped the spokes tight.

"You got a plan?" Trenton yelled at her.

Biting her lower lip, she pointed beyond the bow to the open sea.

"North, northwest. Can you get us to the Marionettes?"

"Never been. Possibly."

"Not good enough."

Trenton glared at her, reaching across and pulling out a rolled-up map from the chart tube on the side of the helm.

"Make him find it. Frau Graves joined them.

"Give him a hand." Sarah Graves ordered.

Frau Graves stabbed the unrolled map on the chart table with the dagger from her belt, just missing Trenton's fingers.

"That's us?" She pointed to a small indentation in the mainland, ignoring his hard gaze.

"That's us."

She traced her black smudged finger across the parchment to the three small islands far to the west. "You can't find *that*?" her voice dripped sarcasm.

"Maybe. I'm just a boiler boy."

"You'll figure it out." She patted his arm and ducked away.

The wounded long boat rode the deep blue hill of the first swell, moving true, but low and struggling, listing to port. The Spanish fort cannons fired another round of chain shot and the crew scattered and dropped. Their aim was accurate, but an over- aggressive amount of powder launched the deadly swirling chain and balls across the top of the fore-deck, tearing out railing but doing no other damage before striking the water thirty yards out.

"Will they pursue?" Sarah Graves shouted.

"Certainly," Trenton yelled back at her.

"Can we get more speed?"

"We can try to run up a jimmy sail."

"Order it!"

"Me? You've got the helm."

Sarah Graves dropped her hands from the wheel spokes

and pressed them to her hips and leaning back, bellowed, "Raise the sail things!"

"Sail *things*?" Trenton grimaced.

"Sir!" Sarah Graves demanded.

"Sail things, *sir*?" He shook his head, reaching around her and taking the spyglass from the helm box.

Sarah Graves pressed back against him, tilting her head so that her raven hair swept his shoulder and extended arm. Feeling her lean into him, Trenton grinned as he raised the spyglass to his good eye, the other side of his face bearing a four-inch knife scar that permanently closed the other.

"The big island on the map doesn't have any city dots," Frau Graves complained.

"Because it's nothing but rock," Trenton shouted over his shoulder, the spyglass turned to the fort.

The one-armed sailor shoved past her carrying a raw-toothed saw across the helm, shouting at Trenton.

"Boiler two needs you! Needle in the red!" With that, he clambered down the steps to assist in clearing the crashed yardarm.

The stern rose, tossing the crew forward as the trawler entered its first deep trough, the face of the approaching swell completely masking the horizon.

"The captain needs eyes to the crow's nest!" Trenton yelled to the struggling crew below. "Look for the Spanish ships!"

Having cleared the harbor rocks and reaching open water, the swells were further spaced and not quite as perilous. The twin engines were proving strong and able, pushing the still-listing long boat farther out into the north-western ocean. Black clouds bringing the midday rains were trudging low in a straight line for them.

"Turn into the storm." Trenton placed his hand on Sarah Grave's, pressing hers to the spoke.

"Turn into the storm, *sir*," she corrected him again.

He rotated the wheel a few inches. She turned it right back.

"We need the cover," he yelled.

"We are *not* changing course!"

"We will if we want to make it to the island, *sir*."

Sarah Graves relented. From high up on the battered mast, a boy screamed down to them.

"Blue flags from the harbor!"

The first crack and flash of lightning shattered the face of the black clouds, blasting blinding white light on the crew, illuminating their determined and frightened faces. The hijacked crew looked like they had serious misgivings over handing over the trawler so easy. With one exception, each sailor on board bore cruel scars and missing limbs from past misadventures. Only Frau Graves was whole, at least on the outside.

The boat continued in its northwestern run, the storm chasing, Sarah Grave's hands locked to the wheel. The coastline at their backs was steep, jungled mountains above the treacherous rocky shoreline. Seabirds were abandoning the open sea for shore, racing low across the wind-swept churning sea. A hard rain began striking the deck.

"That's a lot worse than the daily squall." Trenton pointed, and Sarah Graves stared.

"It'll hide us?" she yelled.

"If it doesn't sink us."

Jagged daggers of heat-lightning arced in all directions, each with a whip crack, stabbing the water and sending up boiling explosions. The jimmy sail on foremast rose but not the mainsail due to the destroyed yardarm. The sea lost all sense of order, sending waves in all directions and batting the boat like a toy, this way and that with frothy explosions of cold foam.

"Must see to that boiler," Trenton yelled in the chaotic winds.

"What do I do with *this*?" Sarah Graves yelled back, her arms straining, her hands locked on the large wheel.

"Keep fighting! Keep the bow aimed. We'll skirt the worst of it."

Turning to plea for help, her wet, tangled hair swept back, revealed her missing ear and the red zigzag scar carved from it to her jaw and throat. Trenton's eyes went wide, seeing the injuries to her otherwise beautiful face for the first time.

"I'll send up the helmsman *if* I find him."

She swung her head around, set her boots out wide for balance, and growled into the streaming wind and rain.

"The Spanish won't take us again."

Entering a deep trough with fifteen-foot walls, the long boat leaned hard on its wounded side, setting off cries of fear and frustration from below. There was a respite of smooth water at the bottom of the basin before the boat climbed the steep face. At the crest, those who were still on their feet stared back to the coast or into the storm.

"Spanish flags," came from high up above.

"Get him down," Sarah Graves ordered a new face on the helm "You, Fat Boy."

"Name's not Fat Boy."

"It is now. I want him down. No more deaths aboard the *Desperation*."

"I'll go," Frau Graves shouted, not waiting for an argument. Jumping from the helm, she started up the mast rungs through the failed cabling and canvas. She climbed without pause even as the mast leaned out hard to port and she had the sea instead of the deck below. Twice, her boots swept and dangled, and twice, she hung on. The rains were brutal, the sky unleashing the hounds of a torrent determined to sweep her away.

A deep and dull concussion carved from the forward hatch and the smokestack aft of the helm belched a plume of gray into the trailing twirl of black exhaust. The wheel in Sarah Graves hands shuddered and twisted at her locked wrists as the signal bells from the helm throttle clanged. The *Desperation* surged forward, scaring the crest of a westward swell as it gained power and speed.

"Trent got it going!" Fat Boy yelled, looking to catch the captain's determined gaze.

She neither heard or acknowledged him, her rain-soaked face raised straight up to the crow's nest sailor and her sister sweeping side to side as they descended.

With the foremast unfurled and both boilers cranking out power, Sarah Graves used the throttle lever and wheel to keep the boat true to course, attacking the watery mountains at an angle that protected the boat's injured side. When waves broke on the foredeck, the punishing water ran the decks, sweeping and toppling crew and stores. Being a quick study, she calculated the angles and speeds necessary to balance the props, rudder, and sails.

The wild-eyed lookout climbed to the helm with Frau Graves, his hand locked on her arm as though her diminutive size and weight could tame his desire to burrow and hide.

"What's the last you saw?" Sarah Graves ignored his quaking expression.

"Two blue flags a mile aft. One turning back."

The full force of the storm came on them like a black fist from hell, turning the sea into madness. Waves from all directions struck the boat, knocking them about.

"All crew below!" Sarah Graves screamed the order.

There was no argument. On the foredeck, the jimmy sail was torn apart into a tangle of rigging and lines. Only Frau Graves remained at her side, one hand clenching the chart she had rolled up fast. Half kneeling, she slid on the slick boards as the boat was lashed onto its port side.

Seeing her still up on deck, Sarah Graves frowned and took one hand off a spoke and balled it in a fist in her younger sister's soaked and filthy coat. She pulled her roughly to her feet and held tight.

"Both your hands on the throttle, need mine to steer," she yelled.

"Are we knackered?"

"Probably, but not yet, so work the lever at my command."

Their fortune was made by sailing for the side of the riotous storm. Battered and low in the water, the long boat rode out the worst, the sisters working together to keep her afloat.

The sky darkened as the fiery sun sank with a flash of sickly green on the uneven horizon. One by one, the crew reappeared, dazed and amazed. The deck was a tumult of wares and fallen sails. They fought their way to their stations as the last of the harsh rain sliced at their skin. The injured *Desperation* limped through the swells to the west.

"What are they up to?" Sarah Graves pointed to a pair of beefy girls. One of them was cranking the wheel on a crane, turning a long wood arm to the other, who was sorting through nets and floats.

"Fish crew saving what's left of their gear," the lookout explained. "It's all they have to earn their keep."

A swing lantern was lit two steps back from the helm. Another was lit on the deck below, above the girl working the crane. She was missing four fingers, using the remaining pad and a well-muscled thumb. The girl at the nets had a shaved head, her skin and scalp covered with red craters. Purple veins connected the open boils. A third girl joined them, her milky blank eyes aimed straight up to heaven as she expertly welded a cleaver on a deck table, chopping chum fish from a covered cask with a square hole.

"No fishing tonight," Sarah Graves yelled from the helm "You'll still be paid," she added, to the lookout's approval.

With the waning daylight, the seas calmed to slow rollers that worked the long boat as they ran to the west, the mainland no longer visible.

"Crew is hungry," Trenton stepped from the shadows. "I'll have those three put a meal together." Without waiting for approval, he called down. "You three, to the galley. Set out hardtack and salted mackerel."

"Thank you for the boiler repair." Sarah Graves rested a free hand on Trenton's shoulder.

With a shrug, he told her, "Boat's got power. Now, about a course?"

"A tasty sprinkling." Frau Graves was pointing eastward to the night's first stars.

"Believes they are sugar granules." Sarah Graves looked to Trenton.

"We're close to losing the forward bilge." Trenton was eyeing her warm, filthy hand on his shoulder. "I should see to it."

"Will the goats be okay?" Frau Graves turned to him, her lovely, intelligent eyes worried.

"Will be if I get on it."

"Then go," she instructed, matter of factly.

"In a moment, yes. Captain?" he turned to Sarah Graves. "Are we still on course for the Marrionettes?"

"I can climb," the wild-eyed lookout offered.

"*The goats*," Frau Graves insisted.

"The island," Trenton pressed.

"I saw a bad haircut," Frau Graves said in calmer voice.

Sarah Graves turned to her sister, whose face was warmed in amber lantern glow.

"What are you talking about?" Trenton was confused.

"The island looks like a black-haired head," Frau Graves explained.

"Which side?" Sarah Graves pressed.

"Is the left side the port side?" the six-year-old asked.

"Yes, my dearie, it is."

"Bad haircut?" Trenton asked.

Ignoring him, Sarah Graves ordered the lookout, "Yes, climb." He dashed down from the bridge and reappeared a moment later, his hands and feet pumping up the mast rungs.

"The haircut?" Trenton tried one last time.

"*Save my goats!*" Frau Graves yelled at him in frustration and anger.

Trenton was startled by her tone. Stepping back from her, he headed below.

"Look for any light," Sarah Graves called up the mast, spinning the wheel hard to port.

"A sugar light," Frau Graves added, yelling upward.

"You saw a lantern on the head?" Sarah Graves asked her sister while squinting hard into the fading light, studying the black swells.

"Middle of the head," Frau Graves answered.

Staring hard out to sea, Sarah Graves willed herself to spot the island.

"I'm hungry!" Frau Graves announced to the entire boat.

"Go below. Bring me something as well."

Hooking her arm in Fat Boy's, Frau Graves dragged him off the helm. "Lead the way. Bet you know."

Trailing a stream of black smoke with spiraling embers, the *Desperation* chugged across the sea, its decks tilted, the wounded ribs raised.

"Anything?" Sarah Graves yelled skyward to the lookout.

"Not yet!"

The clearing sky was making space for increased winds

free of rain for the first time. Sarah Graves wiped the scared side of her face and eyes with her coat cuff. Her eyes were tearing from the strain of staring into the darkening distance over the bow.

Frau Graves and Fat Boy climbed up to her side, both chewing greedily.

"What's that?" Sarah Graves asked, seeing the bone of meat in each of their grimy paws.

"Goat arm." Frau Graves took another bite of freshly charred meat, worked her teeth, and swallowed, "It's from a dead one," she added, taking an object from the pocket of her soaked and dirty coat, "Here you go."

"That is?"

"A potato, are you dim?"

Fat Boy chuckled and nearly choked, his cheeks full of flame-blackened meat.

"The handsome boy almost has the pump working." Frau Graves took another bite of stringy goat meat.

Sarah Graves took a bite of potato and chewed with clear distaste.

After taking her last bite, Frau Graves handed the half eaten bone to her, saying, "I'll climb and go look, too."

"Stay with me," Sarah Graves ordered, giving a worried glance at the mast rungs running in a row up into the night sky.

Frau Graves pretended not to hear, shrugging her shoulders with her eyes seaward. Trenton climbed to the bridge with a salted fish in one hand and a wooden cup of water in the other.

"The fore bilge is dying, there's little to be done. This cursed boat is both haunted and tired. Been thinking…"

"*Oh, no,*" Fat Boy braved.

Trenton ignored that. "Why the island? Why not true

north to the Americas? We're doomed out here. We might make safe waters in three days."

"Because in the morning, the seas will be crawling with Spaniards."

"So, you somehow plan to hide the boat and find a cave on that rock?"

"No cave. No hiding."

"Then, you've lost me."

"Not yet, I haven't." She placed her hand on his shoulder.

"Then what's your plan?" His tone softened as he eyed her touch on his shirt.

"I see red!" Frau Graves yelled from halfway up the mast, "Red like a cherry!"

"Details!" Sarah Graves yelled back.

"Well, it's still red. *Hello.*"

"That's it!" Sarah Graves yelped in satisfaction. Looking up, she called, "Point, my dearie!"

"There's a light on the island?" Trenton interrupted. "We all know that haunted rock is uninhabited."

"*Was.* There's a small encampment. Set up last fall." Sarah Graves turned the wheel in the direction of her sister's small pointed finger.

In the rolling black swells, the island appeared in short glimpses, a distant rise of rock.

"No longer a haircut. The island is a black cake!" Frau Graves called down.

An hour passed, captain and crew staring past the rocking bow.

The swells were forming into waves as they entered the shallows, adding white explosions at the base of the rocky coastline.

"There's no way in," Trenton warned. "We'll be smashed and drowned."

"We'll run the coast until we find a way. I'm turning for the east side."

"Why eastward? Why not the west?"

"A dice toss. Hoping the lee side will be less dangerous."

"Brilliant, we can sink and drown in calmer seas."

Sarah Graves scowled, baring her teeth. "You have a better plan?" she growled and took her hand off him.

Trenton glanced at his barren shoulder, looking wounded before turning his squinting eyes to the uninviting black cliffs. For as far as he could see, there was no change in hue indicating a change of terrain. Sucking in his lips before speaking, he stared Sarah Graves in the eyes.

"Might I suggest, *sir*, that we enter the lee as you ordered but wait out the night before attempting a landing?"

"We can't wait all night," she dismissed him. "The Spaniards will blast us."

"The seas are running high. We must wait for the tides and dawn's light."

"*Must?*" she scoffed.

"Any attempt on that rock now is gambling on certain death."

"Set out the lifeboat to tow and double the lookouts. We'll run for shore if they spot us."

"Madness, *sir*. Your crew isn't one for becoming shark feed."

Displeased and frustrated, Sarah Graves scanned the island's silhouette two hundred yards off. It was so close. Turning the spokes, she aimed the *Desperation* to the island's western side. "I'll decide on the landing. When and where. Don't you need to go see to your engine things?"

"They're being coaled and the needles are fine. I have the bilges manned. We've enough steam to get us to our deaths."

"Then go do something besides paint pictures of our demise."

Wounded by her tongue, Trenton stepped down from the helm. "I'll work on the damaged forward bilge. Perhaps the goats can swim."

"Yes, step to it, save the goats," Frau Graves told him. She climbed onto the chart table, holding a rope for balance, searching the black island for another sighting of the red lantern.

"We must get to shore, to the field, not flounder all night between the rocks and the Spanish," Sarah Graves measured out her displeasure.

"Maybe the soldiers who lit the light built a dock?"

Sarah Graves turned to her.

"In your flowery dreams." She shook her head. Seeing her sister's scowl, she added, "Sorry. Might be."

"It's okay. I found the captain's quarters. Bet there's lots of shiny there." Frau Graves climbed down and headed below, leaving Sarah Graves to her worries as she navigated the boat along the west side of Isla de Marrionettes.

Another hour passed before a safe harbor was spotted on the north lee of the island's only peninsula, a broken finger of crusted outcroppings. Sarah Graves pulled the throttle lever back. Responding to the idling of the engines, Trenton came up top. Searching the tamed swells playing hide and seek with the rocky shore, he spoke respectfully.

"Anchors, sir?" he asked, watching the waves wash the island fifty yards over the port rail.

"Yes. And kill the lanterns."

Trenton yelled down, "Drop the fore and aft anchors!"

Turning to Sarah Graves, he told her, "Bilge two is clear. For now. It won't hold for long. The worst of the hull damage is repaired, and your tiny companion has commandeered the captain's quarters."

"Good," she replied. "Get the lookout back up in the nest looking for the lanterns from those Spanish ships."

21

"Yes, sir. Shall you rest? Perhaps the navigator's bunk? I can take the helm. If we're to die, best done in our dreams."

"They'll be no dying tonight. I'm staying right here." She turned and followed his downward gaze.

"A blanket then? Brew you some tea if I can find it?"

"Eyes off my teats, you. You're burning a hole in my dress. Wipe the wolf's gaze off your face and go do something important."

Trenton turned his wounded eyes to the helm steps and stomped away, leaving her studying the threatening and hungry island face with its dangerous rocks and crags. The rains had returned, drops beading her hands on the spokes. The lantern glowed over her shoulder as it swung back and forth.

Raising her eyes, she searched the top of the black island for a glimpse of that cherry red light.

"I'll find you, and you'll carry us away," she swore.

Fade to black

CHAPTER 2

Film Title: Rascals – The Sequel
Production Day: Two

*I*n the dark blue light an hour before dawn, the waves broke against the rocks with booming explosions. The tide was running low, revealing the encrusted barnacles that spread like an ugly plague on the boulders.

"A tea and biscuit for our captain." Fat Boy climbed up to Sarah Graves at the helm.

"Where's my sister?"

"Light's out in the middle of the other captain's great bed. Shall I wake her?"

"At your deadly peril, no."

Trenton came up the port steps, his face, hands, and arms coal blackened and streaked with sweat. "We have an hour before first light. The aft bilge just failed. I've no more gaskets."

"We go now. Take the wheel. I'll go rustle my little one."

"Sir, if I may—"

"You *may* not. You…" she turned to Fat Boy standing at her side with a wooden cup and biscuit, "… tell every crew member they're to carry provisions. I'm ordering crew and goats lowered to the lifeboat."

"There's a rough quay," Trenton spoke under the extended spyglass. "Looks beaten and unstable. Like we'll ever reach it."

"Give me that." Sarah Graves put her hand out. "Do your spirits always drag an anchor?"

Not listening for his response, she squinted into the raised spyglass, "If only they had built docking. No matter, we go."

A quarter-hour later, all the crew was up on deck, including Frau Graves in a snarling mood, having been stirred from a dreamy slumber. The dull silver light of dawn bore through the eastern clouds. The rolling, listing long boat was struggling, both bilges having given up their ghosts. On the main deck, the crew and their hastily filled sacks stood among the baying and skittering seven remaining goats.

"Our dead, sir?" one of the three fisher girls called from the steps of the helm.

"They go over first. Drape them if need be but make it quick. Then those goats to the boat. They'll be… reluctant."

"Reluctant, sir? They'll surely maim whoever tries."

"Then, you're my girl, even if you've only six fingers."

"Aye, Captain."

"There won't be room for all." Trenton pointed to their lone, open hull skiff riding the swells alongside.

"We'll make do."

"Perhaps you and I should attempt a landing first. Come back for them?"

"There will be no return. The Spanish will see to that."

"Yes, but I…"

"Goats, first!" Sarah Graves called, turning from Trenton. "Pack them in tight. Bind them if need be."

The three fisher girls went to work at their crane, lowering the animals one at a time.

Without ceremony but a fast-muttered prayer, the three dead shipmates were raised over the seaward rail and dropped—one killed by flying wagon parts, one killed by musket fire, and the last fallen into the transmission.

The listing *Desperation* was struggling in the rolling sea, its lower hull filling with water down below. With the wild eyed and baying goats pressed forward in the boat and half contained with fishing net, it was clear there wasn't room for all the crew and their grain sacks of supplies.

"I knew this would happen." Trenton pointed out as four sailors climbed over the side to the rope ladder.

"Some will swim. I will." Sarah Graves cut back at him, "Can you?"

"Would if I could. Never learned."

"And you call yourself a sailor?"

"A coaler."

Looking to the rest of her crew on the deck below, she called to them. "I need volunteers for the oars. Those who can swim will hang on alongside."

Sheepish eyes turned to the waves smashing the rocks.

"A fistful of gold for all swimmers!"

No hands were raised.

"Three, now four blue flags to the south," the lookout called from the crow's nest.

"Get him down," she ordered Trenton.

Instead of obeying, he climbed to the deck and walked to the shoreward rail.

"I'll swim for you," Frau Graves offered, frowning at the violent waves blasting the logs supporting the quay.

"There you go!" Sarah Graves shouted, "It's not far at all."

"Cannon fire!" came from the crow's nest.

The boat shuddered, the bow struck with a flaming explosion of timber. Sarah Graves was hurled from the helm as the mast took a vicious and terminal direct hit. It's seventy-five feet of hardwood arched back, its mountings failing. Rigging and the remaining yardarm crashed across the helm, followed by the dying scream and thud of the look-out's body.

Rising from her hands and knees, Sarah Graves lifted her sister by the scruff of her collar and dragged her across the planks to the rail. In the waters below, the skiff was packed full with the frightened and crying crew. Trenton and Fat Boy were manning the oars. The lifeboat rode dangerously low in the water, struggling to make safe distance from the floundering and burning *Desperation*.

The last two still aboard were Sarah and Frau Graves, except for the fallen lookout lying dead in a pool of blood and sea spray. They climbed over side by side and dropped to the waters.

The lifeboat was battered by the waves as it was rowed to shore. Reaching the rocks and the man-made quay, Trenton launched a line at a post up above. The second was thrown from the stern by Fat Boy. Both boys struggled and cried out in effort, pulling the small craft within reach of the level planks. The crew climbed out fast with much confusion, small hands clenching for purchase on any handhold they could find.

Frau Graves swam to the rear of the lifeboat and climbed up into it. Soaked and coughing up seawater, she freed the terrorized goats from the tangled fence of fishing net, getting knocked onto her rear. The panicked goats bounded out, needing no encouragement. The lifeboat rose in the face of a wave poised to break. Grasping a barnacled cross beam, she hung on tightly as the wave exploded. Her hands torn free, she splashed into the water and twisted this way and that in the churn. She surfaced kicking, spitting, and gagging.

"Come, climb!" her sister shouted from above.

Seeing the stone steps leading up and out of the water, she swam for them. Climbing onto the first step, the next wave broke, knocking her hard against the steps. As the wave retreated, it tried to suck her back with it. Fighting the pull by locking her hands on the sides of the coarse stone, she kicked her legs and started up. Her sister's outstretched hands grabbed her and pulled.

Up on level ground, she remained on her knees, her arm around her sister. Turning around and looking out to sea, there was their large boat, smoking and sinking. The *Desperation* went under bow first, its stern in flames, timbers splintering. She turned away, no second look, and followed her sister, joining the straggling line of the crew across the rocks.

Twenty yards in, there was nothing but the rocky terrain. The sailors spread out, each searching for any possible cover. Frau Graves huddled low on the gray rocks and called out to the scattering goats.

"There you go. Enjoy your new home."

The drenched and battered crew came back together and sat down in a circle, heads down, their clothing filthy and torn, their eyes to the rocks between their feet. With failing strength but determination pasted on her face, Sarah Graves strode purposefully to the forlorn sailors.

"Catch your wind, collect yourselves, then we move out."

Glaring at her under tangled hair, Trenton wiped seawater from his handsome scarred face and called over.

"Our captain loses our boat but still wants us to follow? Where now, *savior*?" This last growled with a cruel edge.

Stricken by his cutting words, she looked to the others, all faces lowered.

"I've heard that on the north side there are trees for cover."

"She *heard*," one of the fishing girls dismissed with thick sarcasm.

The others' voices muttered low over the rocks and their feet.

"I'll go," Frau Graves said. "Are the trees near the field?"

"Believe so, yes, And fresh water. We can build a fire."

At that, three heads rose and scanned the sea to the south, none looking in the direction of the sunken trawler.

"The Spaniards will find us and cut us down," a wet voice quaked with unveiled fear.

"No," Sarah Graves countered. "They saw the boat go under. Those cowards will turn tail to go celebrate their great sea victory."

"So she says," another grumbled.

Turning away, Sarah Graves searched for any trail markers across the sun-blasted, rocky terrain that reached out to the west and north. Besides low tufts of scrub grass, there was nothing else to see except a steep hill to her far left.

"A fire? Your word is good for that?" another spoke, gathering up her soaked sack of supplies.

"I nicked the captain's firebox," Frau Graves added, "It's in Fat Boy's sack."

"No more than a mile, maybe two," Sarah Graves dangled encouragement. "Dry your clothing, cook a meal."

"Lunacy," Trenton mumbled, "...but I'm in." He got to his feet.

The others did as well, and with Sarah Graves taking the lead, Frau Graves followed to the northern climb.

The mile-long trek was a slow one, all of them stumbling across the rocks. As the sun climbed up into the blue sky, it broiled the island. They walked in a ragged line with Frau Graves having taken the lead. From time to time, she would sing.

> *"My goats are happy,*
> *My goats are safe,*
> *There's just enough grass,*
> *On this forsaken place."*

Coming to the base of the hill, Sarah Graves stopped and called out.

"We should set up camp."

They were at the crest of a ravine that ran to the waves and rocks in the western waters. There were a few capomo trees and some scraggly vegetation.

No one objected, and half an hour later, a fire crackled in a circle of stones. Each of them took something to eat from their sacks and placed it on a shared flat rock.

Tinned meat was cooked along with green potatoes and salted cod. The crew ate their first meal in the shade as a clinging humidity slicked their tired, dirty faces. A cloud of mosquitos found them and took to their skin, buzzing and stabbing.

Quickly and greedily finishing his meal, Fat Boy gathered fallen tree limbs rich with green mold for the fire. Trenton got up as well, cursing and waving at the insects. Using the knife from his belt, he chopped palm fronds and laid them out over the fire, eliciting wails and threats in response to the low greasy smoke.

"It'll slacken their appetites," he explained, smashing an unknown flying insect with the flat of his hand.

The day grew hot. Water was collected in the meat tins from a meager stream feeding the ravine.

"Take your coat, sir? You must be a sweaty mess," Fat Boy offered Sarah Graves.

"No, as in never, same for her." She gestured to Frau Graves.

The boy looked confused. Both girls were slick with perspiration under the weight of their heavy coats.

"Rest or sleep," Sarah Graves told the others. "We'll head out at nightfall."

"For the little one's big red cherry lantern?" the six-fingered fisher girl asked, her voice conflicted by hope and confusion.

"Exactly, yes, for our escape."

When the sun set, the only light was from the glowing fire pit embers.

"Before we follow you another step, what in God's name is your next plan for our gruesome deaths?" Trenton stabbed at the fire with a branch.

"Taking all who wish to go to the Americas," Sarah Graves answered in a firm voice.

"I'm at a loss. You've pirated us onto a large rock in the middle of the ocean, sunk our boat, and—"

"I know my words don't yet have any sway with you. You'll have to wait and see. And trust. You, others, rest up," She scowled at Trenton before looking as kindly as she could muster to the remaining crew. "For those willing to trust me, you'll be away from this island before moon fall."

"Why would we follow you another step?" the one-armed sailor pressed.

"Follow me, and I promise you a renewed and rich life."

"Rich? As in riches?" Fat Boy's round face brightened with wonder.

"Beyond your most fanciful dreams. Banquets and home-steads and more."

"I'm in. Roasted pig for breakfast. Pie and beer for dinner."

"Then loan me your trust a while longer, a few days."

The others eyed her with skepticism and fear, their faces lit by the fading fire.

"That westward wind Hastings told you about? The Niñas?" Frau Graves asked, sounding hopeful. "That'll be our saving grace, right?"

"Yes, the El Niño, my little one. Thank you, and that's right."

Looking to the east, she saw there was no moonlight to help light the way forward.

"Rise, everyone, we go now. Gather your sacks and form a line. Quietly, please." She stirred the sailors to their feet. A current of salt air swept up the ravine and through the camp, nudging their backs inland. The remaining crew of ragtag sailors formed a loose queue, only Trenton holding back. He was stacking branches on the nearly dead fire.

"We'll need the light to find our way back," he countered her impatient and disapproving glare.

"There's no need. Leave that and like the others, hush up and march."

After climbing the northern hill, the crew of the *Desperation* hunched low in jungle vegetation and watched a hand lantern cross a fifty-acre clearing. They were hiding at the edge of a military encampment and airfield on the central plateau of Isla de Marrionettes. There was a low thatched building off to the left of the field where a second light shone through the doorway. Male voices carried from the building.

The hand-held lantern at first looked like it was starting to fly, rising straight up. The hunkering sailors watched the light ascend, its flame revealing the plank rungs of a ladder.

A hundred feet up, a wick was lit inside a pan circled by

panes of red glass. The fire blossomed as the soldier climbed down, the tinted glass on top of the tower glowing brightly.

"Merry and cherry red," Frau Graves gushed in delight.

"What's *that*?" Fat Boy pointed off to the side of the tower, his voice full of wonder.

Ignoring him, Frau Graves took her sister's hand and asked, "The winds?"

"With us, as Hastings promised."

Beyond the tower, the high red lantern light reflected off a curved, ribbed, canvas. The massive egg-shape was raven black on its nether sides.

"Can we go now?" Frau Graves pleaded. "It's half a sweet melon."

"No, lovey, we must wait until the cottage light goes out."

The hand lantern reached the low grass and crossed to the small building and entered.

"What's that?" Trenton pointed to the strange, large shape.

"You'll see when we get moonlight. You good with knots?" she asked.

"Of course."

Turning to the others, she said, "We'll go as one, save Trenton, who'll cast us off. I'm told there are four lines, one to each side that he'll untie."

"We're going *where*?" the girl with the wormy blisters and boils worried.

"The basket. Each of you find a place inside. It's going to be tight, just like the lifeboat."

"Minus my goats," Frau Graves pouted.

"When Trenton's done, help him in." Sarah Graves continued, "I'll need your help dropping ballast. Clear?"

"Why are we getting inside a basket?" Fat Boy raised the only question.

"It's under the balloon. Are you dim?" Frau Graves

remembered her manners and smiled to remove some of the sting.

Three hours passed before the hut went dark and the field was sprayed with eastern moonlight. With the rising moon, the airship and gondola below were clear to see, as were the four long tether lines.

"No time better than the now." Sarah Graves climbed to her feet, turning to Trenton.

"Work fast and true."

With that, she led the gaggle of weary youths into the wind-brushed grass, all of them running hunched over, trying to stay out of sight. Reaching the gondola, they climbed in one at a time. As they lowered to the sides of the thatched basket, Sarah Graves busied herself with the memorized priming of the gas flame feed, not striking a match yet.

"We'll gain sky over the island before I light it," she explained to all the staring eyes around her.

Each time a tether was released, the rectangular basket leaned away from the freed side. With the fourth line dropped, the aircraft tiled with the wind and skidded along the field, clouting rocks. Trenton climbed over and spilled to the floor, pleased with his efforts. His pleasure was muted by Sarah Graves saying to him, "Took your time about it. You're the tallest. Heave the ballasts over."

With each eighty pounds of shot and rocks dumped over, the balloon rose. Others did their best to assist as the balloon climbed into an eastward breeze that turned into winds fifty yards up in the sky.

"Lights!" Wormy Girl yelled, standing at the back corner.

Two lanterns exited the doorway of the building down below, followed by shouts. Seconds later, several rifles fired. With nowhere to hide, the youths tried their best for cover by balling up against the thatching.

Ignoring the gunfire and angry shouting soldiers, Sarah

Graves lit the fuel burner. A burst of hot burning gas blew back, singeing her hair on the ruined side of her face. Ignoring that, she cranked the feed valve and adjusted the two gas pressure levers. The balloon rose faster as the blue and gold flames streamed upward.

Bullets pierced the basket's underside. There were no cries, no screams from anyone being hit. Two hundred yards up, the aircraft was grasped by the eastern current and carried away from the airfield. Within minutes, they passed over the east edge of the black island, sailing in the direction of the mainland.

At daybreak, they were crossing the endless Mexican landscape three hundred yards below. The air channels had shifted with the effect of the hot terrain, turning them north. Fat Boy and the six-fingered girl used a section of patching canvas tied to the sides to provide some wavering shade. The gondola had by then been fully explored. They had found potted water, a primitive medical kit, a map, and chart locker. From a strong box, they unwrapped a long musket and two flintlock pistols as well as a few bayonets and battle knives.

Having stood watch through the endless night, Sarah Graves nodded off, caught herself, wiped sleep spittle from her lips, and clasped the balloon controls.

"You're exhausted," Trenton spoke from the corner of the gondola where he had sulked through the night beside a water cask. "Let me spell you."

"I'm still able, but... thank you."

"Know where we are?" Fat Boy untangled himself from the press of bodies in the opposite corner and groggily climbed to his feet. He eased toward Frau Graves, who was greedily eating a piece of rock candy secreted in her coat pocket. The rest of the crew was asleep, except for Wormy

Girl and her tongueless shipmate whom their prior captain had renamed Liar.

"Can I have another look?" Fat Boy asked, his bare feet tripping up in the maze of legs and tilted heads. Unintentionally bumping into Frau Graves, he received a hot-fired elbow from her.

"Sure. I might just promote you to ship's navigator."

Sarah Graves opened her coat and took out a rolled map from the lining pocket. She secured it from the winds to the small chart table with the four spring clasps binding the useless military charts below.

"We're approximately here." She drew a large circle with her finger, inches below a wandering row of red-inked Xs. Those marked their northern route and the vital fuel resupply posts.

Frowning at the vague circling of her finger, he placed his chubby hand flat and measured the distance to the first X. "Would help if the map had a legend. Know the distances?"

"I was told we're to drop for fuel two days out."

"Little to go on." Fat Boy rubbed his nose, his eyes steady on the crudely sketched details on the map. "What's this skinny breakfast loaf?"

"The Sierra Nevada. We're parallel to it as you can see."

Trenton appeared at their side to have a look. "Looks drawn by a drunkard," he grumbled. Getting a knife-flick glare from Sarah Graves, he backpedaled, "But workable. This area..." he tapped the top of the map, "... Americas?"

Sarah Graves answered with the glint of a smile.

"Really? *Really?*" Fat Boy leaned close, his chin inches from the parchment.

"Yes, really," she delivered more delight.

"The Americas," Trenton pondered, looking over the basket rim to the flat brown terrain stretching out forever before them.

"Thank you, sir." He offered her a rare heartfelt smile.

"May I?" Fat Boy took a sliver of coal chalk from the ink well on the side of the table.

"You're our navigator."

He traced the same circle she had drawn with her fingertip. After a moment's consideration of the map's other sparse terrain details, he advised, "When these mountains are in sight, we'll angle to the left here." He tapped the inked cluster of circles resembling plateaus.

"Well done, yes." Sarah Graves squeezed his shoulder, lighting a pleased smile in his round, pink face. "If you two can work together…" she turned to Trenton and tilted her head, "… I'm going to close my eyes for a few winks."

A hot draft of rushing air from the woven floor of the gondola raised the hem of her coat and dress. Frau Graves had opened the small wicker hatch and was maneuvering over it in a squat.

"Gotta poop, sir," she let out a jingle of laughter.

After two quick grunts, she spun and giggling, looked down through the opening, watching her dropping sail downward fast.

"Direct hit, sir," she bubbled, falling in her mirth.

"That's disgusting." Trenton shook his head, but the smile on his one-eyed, handsome face belied the words.

"I'm saving my next for California." Frau Graves closed and latched the door.

Lowering beside her, Sarah Graves stroked her sister's hair. "It's a fine plan." She pressed her lips to the child's temple before reclining back into the shade and closing her eyes.

Fade to black

36

CHAPTER 3

Film Title: Rascals – The Sequel
Production Day: Three

$\mathscr{N}$ine days later, Sarah Graves slid a leather envelope back inside the lining pocket of her long coat after handing over payment for the new fuel canisters, fresh water cask, food stock, and six hay-scented horse blankets for the increasingly cold nights. The transaction was carried out in English, unlike the two prior drops on the red Xs.

As the crew loaded the supplies into the gondola, Fat Boy called from the helm, "Saw that coming, sir." He pointed to the east side of the military and trading post, past the decrepit oxen corral.

The two fishing girls were furtively dashing with their heads low, passing the wagon shop abutting the smoking doorway of the blacksmith.

"Damn it all, but can't blame them." Trenton had his good

eye on the two crew members moving out beyond the low buildings and out onto the wagon trail. "Want me to stop them?"

"No, let them go," Sarah Graves shook her head. "It's their gambit. Let's get aloft before anyone else gets clever and stupid."

She was the last to clamber up into the basket. The remaining crew continued their familiar tasks to get afloat, dumping ballast sacks while Trenton and the six-fingered girl cast off the tether ropes. The balloon climbed smooth and fast, Sarah Graves adjusting the burners. Five minutes later, they were a hundred yards up.

As sunset turned the landscape a burnt orange, the wind-swirled gondola drew within miles of the foothills before the base of the Sierra Nevada mountains. For the next hour, the balloon glided across the sky.

"What are these?" Trenton held his palm up.

"Almost funny," Frau Graves brushed the first drops of rain from her brow.

Worrying over the Hasting's map in the blue light of the burner flames, Fat Boy held a bit of chalk in his hand.

"How do we turn the basket further west?" He turned to Sarah Graves.

Seeing that she was nodding off while still on her feet, he studied the mountain range with stolen glances to the map. "Guess the currents will do it," he said, no one else paying him any mind.

When darkness was complete, he had no idea which side of the mountains they were floating to. Sarah Graves had begrudgingly laid down in the crowded basket alongside her sister, who was rolled up in a fetal ball. At the helm for the night, he stayed on his feet, eyes to the map in the blue flame light.

At dawn, the dark eastern sky was stroked with purple.

Fat Boy's head was jerking alert every couple of minutes, his knees fading as he fought to remain awake. Three hundred yards off, deep lavender bluffs stood tall and steep. Sarah Graves found her feet and pushing Fat Boy aside, studied the map before squinting into the faint western sky.

"How did this happen?" She struggled to awaken, shaking her sleepy head and rubbing her eyes.

"What's wrong?" Fat Boy asked.

After scanning the western sky again, she pointed to the map.

"We're here." She pressed her finger to the parchment.

"No, we can't be," he answered, but his voice was uncertain. "I thought to wake you."

"And you didn't?" We're on the wrong side."

"I thought the currents would—"

"You're our navigator. We needed the western side."

"What can we do?"

"There's nothing *to do* but cobble a new plan." She turned away. The snowcapped Sierras climbed to them in their rising, northward march.

A frigid wind buffeted the gondola. She pulled the horse blanket from her shoulders and draped in over Fat Boy's back, whispering, "No word to the others until I say."

"I'm sorry, I—"

Looking skyward, she glared at the churning clouds. Spiraling snowflakes were falling.

By midday, their world and sky were frosted white. The balloon was passing over treetops and granite cliff faces. The balloon climbed, helped by the thin frigid air, sailing a hundred yards above the nearly vertical mountainside. Having connected a fresh fuel canister, Sarah Graves adjusted the valves and knobs, frustrated time and again by the sputtering blue hissing flames.

"It's the thin air, or we were sold watered fuel." She

twisted as hard as she could on the tank valve, fighting to keep the fires at an even burn. While the huddled crew bit and chewed hardtack, Trenton stood and squinted into the northwest distance.

"Tell me you're not going to attempt to cross? We'll never gain the altitude."

"Was planning to, yes. Now I'm struggling to keep us aloft."

The white crowns of hundred-foot pine trees lined the ascending bluff. An iced white lake was forward to the north, shaped like an infant sleeping on its side.

"Should we land before night falls?" Trenton frowned at Sarah Graves, plying the valves and cursing under her breath. "We can't risk flying blind, not with that." He pointed to the unsteady flow of blue flame. Up above, the balloon canvas was sagging, the ropes pressing deep grooves.

"We're pressing on." She turned her back on him. "Go forward with Fat Boy, use the spyglass. Do something useful."

Taken aback by her tone, he pulled his hand back. He had hoped to rest it on her shoulder, a gesture of caring. He kept his hurt eyes to her, hoping for a bit of affection. Getting none, he climbed through the arms and legs and heads crowded under shared horse blankets.

The change from evening to total dark came fast, the gray sky going black with little warning. Freezing air clenched the crew, who pressed together for warmth, shivering in the dark with only the faltering blue-tipped flame light. Flying blind, Sarah Graves was the only one standing as Trenton and Fat Boy gave up on the spyglass.

An hour into the black night, a hundred-foot tree loomed silently. It struck the basket with a *crack*, knocking it onto its side. Toppled from her feet, Sarah Graves was down on all fours among the frantic screams and scampering of her terrified crew. Frau Graves dug her fingers into her sister's coat arm and yanked hard, pulling her away from the splintering hole in the floor and side. The gondola was hit again and tipped over, the crew screaming and clawing for handholds. The hole in the thatched flooring opened wider. Sarah Graves grasped the steel legs of the controls and climbed to her feet. She found the leather handle to the rip line and pulled on it for all she was worth, opening the landing vent high up in the darkness. The parachute valve on the inflated silk tore open and the balloon began to descend.

"What are you doing? Not here!" Trenton yelled.

"We've no choice. It's either land or spill to the rocks or whatever's below."

The basket was smashed by an unyielding limb, tipping it over on its side. Dashed against the controls, Sarah Graves hit her head hard, taking a harsh, stunning blow. Her forehead gashed, and her vision blurred. She gathered her wits and pulled the second rip line with all her might, opening it all the way.

With hot gasses rushing out, their descent accelerated. The silk above was stabbed by a second tree limb. The balloon sagged, pouring out hot hissing air. The aircraft began a spiraling fall. Knocked side to side, the gondola was bashed again, this time with an explosion of snow that fell inside. The crew was crying and screaming, each trying to claw for something, anything to hold on to.

The gondola struck an outcropping, the jarring impact turning it over. The youths tumbled out into the unknown below. Smacking tree limbs and screaming, their bodies were knocked this way and that as they fell like tossed rag dolls. Their fall was broken time and again as faces and bodies struck hardwood.

They landed in a scatter, their bodies crunching through the iced roof of a snowdrift. Battered by impact with the ice crust, they sank deep into soft snow underneath, striking hidden rocks. The gondola followed, torn free from the silk hung up in the treetops, falling upside down, spilling their meager supplies.

Those who could climb out, did so. Others were dragged through tunnels made by digging and kicking. Six Fingers was unconscious, her temple sliced open to the bone in the bloody tangle of hair. Sarah Graves had landed beside her. Brushing the snow and blood from the girl's wound, she kicked her way forward through the frozen white powder, her hands gripping the girl's bloody collar as she pulled her to open air.

One by one, the other survivors appeared, digging with freezing hands, bashing the snow aside, gulping air. Those who could stand saw they were on the edge of the knoll at the base of a ravine. Ten yards off, a massive oak tree blocked the snowfall. They staggered and crawled to the dirt and rocks underneath it, each crossing to the island of dirt surrounded by a world of white. They gathered against the trunk of the tree, Sarah Graves the last to join them, dragging Six Finger's limp body.

Frau Graves found her feet and crossed the dirt rocks to help her sister. The two of them pulled Six Fingers to the tree and reclined her against it. Others leaned in to examine their injured friend in the darkness, wiping her tangled hair aside. A sleeve was torn and wrapped around the wound. Sarah Graves looked away, her head down, to the steep snow-filled ravine.

"I'm so sorry." Her words formed a white cloud.

Trenton pulled himself up on unsteady feet, freezing hands in his pockets, looking to the drift that had broken their fall.

"I'm going for the basket," he said to anyone who might hear. "We need the rifle and whatever else I can find."

"I'll help." Frau Graves stepped around her sister, tripping on a rock in the dirt but catching her fall. "Bet I can find the firebox."

"I dragged out a sack," one of the youths said.

"Same here. Don't know how," another added.

Looking to the remaining survivors huddled before the tree trunk, Sarah Graves spoke to them. 'Well, done, all of you. We're not finished yet."

Turning away, she squinted to the drifts. Icy moonlight was beginning to lay across them. To the right, her sister and the Trenton were starting to dig. She knelt beside the stricken Six Fingers to do something useful.

Trenton and Frau Graves dug their tunnel with freezing hands, taking turns while the other breathed life back into red, stinging fingers. Time and again, the snow roof collapsed onto them. Digging themselves out, neither relented. The tunnel was ten feet long after twenty minutes. Shivering, Trenton cursing, their hands going numb, they punched and clawed at the snow with their fists.

An hour later, a crack and spray of ice shards preceded the first view of the gondola being shoved from behind. Filled deep with snow, the damaged basket plowed up soil as it was shouldered into the clearing. The others at the base of the tree got to their feet to help. Together, they went to work, their stinging pink fingers grasping and dragging it toward the large tree, where Sarah Graves watched from beside Six Fingers, her bloody hand pressing the rag.

"Come, child," Trenton called, and Frau Graves appeared from the rear of the gondola, wiping snow from her face and hair. The basket was pushed and pulled forward, clacking on the rocks into the cover of the tree.

"Tip it on its side," Trenton barked, kneeling and sliding his fingers under to lift. Other hands joined in, and the basket crunched onto its side, spilling snow and revealing the two supply boxes bolted to the thatching. Fat Boy climbed in, clawed snow aside, and opened both, handing all he found back to helping hands.

Sarah Graves studied the faces of her small crew, each made ancient by the ghost-white moonlight: Six Fingered Stanton beside her, Trenton, Fat Boy, the one-armed sailor, and the six-year-old girl with her boil-scarred face they were calling Wormy. She looked to the others digging out and searching the gondola. Each small face looked worn out and weary, some eyes to her, pleading. These were her charges, her followers, their fate decided with each decision she made.

"Damn, I don't even know their names," she scolded herself.

"Fat Boy, what's your real name?" she called over.

"James Reed."

"Which do you prefer?

"Neither, sir."

"Okay. How about you?" She pointed to the one-armed child.

"Margaret Reed, sir, and the girl in your arms is Stanton. It's her last name, I think."

That left the boy whose tongue was cut out. She nodded to him, and he replied, "Lewis Kesenberg, but Liar's fine by me." His voice was thick, wet, and garbled.

Beside him was the one-legged boy, who volunteered, "Snyder, sir."

"A fine crew," Sarah Graves said, looking again at each of their faces. Her teeth clicked, her jaw locking as she bit off her fears and doubts. A child bumped into her, gathering wet branches in hope of a fire. Sarah Graves looked up into the cold black sky to the east, to stars beginning to shine like ice diamonds. Snow was no longer falling. Sliding a dirty hand inside her coat, she traced a reassuring fingertip across the two rows of documents in the lining pockets.

Trenton stepped past, juggling head-size rocks in his strong hands and arms. "Your sister found the firebox." He dropped them and pushed them side to side, forming the first curved wall of a fire pit.

"Yes, thank you." Her voice was distant, hesitant.

Reading her tone, he stepped to her side. "Please stand, sir."

She did as he asked. His arms opened, and he gave her a tired smile.

"Bless me with an embrace? It'll help," he offered.

Seeing his concerned, handsome face, she stepped forward slowly.

"I won't bite you," he encouraged.

She stepped into his arms, feeling their strong caress. Closing her eyes, she felt his lips and breath in the tangled hair over her missing ear.

"You're doing fine, sir." His voice was gentle, something she had never heard from him before. She couldn't find words to reply. Closing her eyes, she held onto him a moment longer.

"Back to it." He ended the embrace, adding, "Sir."

"Yes." She stepped back. "Please finish the fire."

One-armed Margaret Reed bumped into them, gathering twigs and leaves. Trenton walked away and Sarah Graves joined in the search for sticks and anything else they could use for kindling.

Inside the tipped gondola, Fat Boy was staring at the pistol in Frau Graves' hand, a lockbox open at their feet

"Know how to fire it?" he asked.

"I know how to load but never fired. She does." She pointed her half-eaten piece of hardtack to her sister.

Fat Boy struck a wood match across the coarse sulfur patch on the side of the firebox tin. Cupping the flame with his other hand, he asked her, "Have anything we can burn?"

Setting the pistol down, she opened her coat and reached inside the lining pocket, regretfully taking out a page of a document. She balled it up and held it into the match flame. Together, they climbed out and joined the others at the growing circle of rocks.

One-armed Margaret Reed used her boot heel to press the last rock into place. A minute later, the hesitant fire came to life, mostly twisting smoke. Liar kneeled and added a few twigs and waved air underneath the small, struggling flame.

"Come to me," he said in his badly mangled voice, the others watching on, willing the fire to grow. He lay a stick across the top and made a pleased gurgling sound as the flame took to it.

The injured Stanton and one-legged Snyder turned away. Kneeling in the rocks and dirt, they scraped the excess salt off two fish from the second supply box. Behind them came the first sound of the crackling fire, along with grateful voices.

"Warm food tonight." Snyder ran a stick through the fish in his hand, and Stanton did the same. Setting those aside, they repeated the process.

Ten minutes later, spiked fish were held over the fire by eager hands. All eyes were to their next meal cooking in the savory smoke, everyone except Frau Graves, who had yet to tire of bland hardtack.

From the east side of the encampment, rocks cracked as though knocked aside. Frozen tree branches snapped, followed by a deep angry growl from low to the ground. All heads turned, staring into the night. More stones were batted in the darkness.

"What's that?" Sarah Graves asked.

"Too big to be a wolf." Trenton set his meal aside.

The second growl was thick with hunger and madness. Drawn to the scent of the cooking oily fish, the beast in the shadows moved closer. In the orange glow of the firelight, all eyes were wide, the youths frozen in fear.

Trenton was the first to move, turning around and grabbing one of the muskets. Sarah Graves watched him through the filthy strands of her hair. As he cocked the flintlock, she spun around and took up one of the pistols.

She rose to her feet alongside Trenton, who took a step forward on cat's feet in the direction of the trashing twenty feet away. Sensing her move to his side, Trenton pulled her back behind himself and stepped out further.

The bear entered the edge of the firelight, its front paws crashing down, shaking the ground, spraying snow. Pulling its lips back and snorting, its five-inch incisors showed thick, yellowed blades ready to tear into flesh.

Trenton took a frightened, hesitant step back, his confidence challenged.

"Get back to the others!" he yelled at Sarah Graves, locking his legs.

Raising the rifle to his squinting good eye, he saw the bear's shoulders arch and head lower, preparing to charge. It let out a deep roar.

Trenton lowered his aim from the bear's head to its wide chest, a larger target. Using the aiming bead at the end of the rifle barrel, he yelled for all he was worth.

"Leave or die!" as if the hungry bear understood his words. The animal gained three times its size as it rose on its hind feet, claws out. Given a clear view of the heart and belly, Trenton pulled the trigger.

The explosion was blinding, the rifle roaring, kicking up after discharging. The crew screamed and scattered, except for Sarah Graves, who remained in place, her stance strong and sure. The bear clambered forward, furious and wounded, its eyes narrowed. It swung a paw of large deadly claws across the air between itself and Trenton, who was already reloading, head down, hands working maniacally.

Sarah Graves raised her pistol and took aim at the bear's head, its open mouth, and gnashing hungry teeth. The bear staggered forward, paws crashing down, shoulders arched, about to charge, bristling to attack. Trenton cocked the musket as the bear started for him, lumbering, picking up speed. He pulled the trigger, sending out another blast of yellow flame as the claws swept the air less than a foot from his chest.

Sarah Graves flinched and jerked an inch, thinking Trenton had been struck. She pulled the trigger, and the recoiling pistol struck her forehead, knocking her from her feet.

Mortally wounded, the bear's last roar was a snarled growl of confusion. It took its final lunge into the firelight, chest splattered with blood. Leaning on one arm, it collapsed sideways, pounding the ground.

Trenton fell the opposite direction, his rifle clacking on the rocks, the back of his head knocked forward. The bear's bloody entrance hole was small. The back of his head had exploded like a red volcano. His face hit the rocks with a splash of blood and brains.

Looking down at the smoking pistol in her hand, Sarah Graves screamed.

Fade to black

CHAPTER 4

Black Curtain

$\mathcal{M}$y name is Florentino Urbino, call me Flor, everyone else does. In the ugly world of movie-making, I'm what's called a fixer, and no one's better at that than me. You're coming along with me, how can you not? I'll lead you up and down the backside of Hollywood, including the nasty parts. Best if you buckle up because we're headed far up the skirt of this machine, our first stop is that day's filming of *Rascals – The Sequel*. Let me pull the black curtain back for you so you can get a better look.

Here we are on the movie set, as usual, with a mess on our hands. In this case, it's Trenton's dead body on the ground, his head a bloody melon.

"What the dog fuck was *that?*" the mouthy Assistant Director yelled with no filter as usual. He was standing beside me, back of Camera Two.

The other forty-seven members of our second-unit film

crew kept their noses to the grindstone, maintaining their unblinking focus on equipment and tasks—all of them obscenely overpaid and overfed. They knew better than to lift until Dice broke the creative spell by shouting, "Cut."

Because *that* word had not yet been called, our cast of child actors remained frozen in their poses and expressions as did the stunned audio, camera, and lighting teams.

Imagine a series of three concentric rings, each one larger than the other and, as always, in the middle —the center of attention, deserved or not—the cast, those *enfants terribles* with their soiled and greedy hearts.

I was in the second ring, amidst the extended boom mics, cameras, lights, and defusing panels, a single step back, a hand's reach away, from the alleged brains of this film, Dice, our Director. Dice, both pretentious and visionary—when lucid—was our second- rate, overwhelmed, in-over-his-head leader. He was crouched to my right beside Camera Three, his eyes aligned with the lens, one hand on the shoulder of Bear the Director of Photography with his aides and writers panting at his back.

Am I jealous of Dice and all his acclaim and awards and reputation as a brilliant, hard-working visionary? You bet I am. Worse, he's in my well-deserved role.

"Cut!" Dice yelled after a fair amount of Trenton's blood had pooled under his face there on the faux snow, dirt, and rocks.

With that single command, the entire film company exhaled. The stunned young actors and actresses turned away from the bloody spectacle before them, to their coaches and minders watching from the outer ring of the set.

Dice stood up from the camera as crew members climbed from their gear and tentatively entered the winter movie set.

"*That* was our twist, our *tortillon dramatique,*" Dice

pronounced in his usual grandiose voice as lights, audio, and cameras were powered down.

In this mess of an underfunded production—no fault of mine—my place in the circles was wherever in the hell I feel like. Sod the circles of importance. *I* got the checks written, *I* groped and licked the investors, *I* kneed and cooed the talent, and *I* made this cinematic magic happen.

As the *oh-so-important* lines of the circles dissolved, the Assistant Director took brief command of the motley gang. His nickname 'Touch' was well-deserved, although *touched* was more accurate.

"Cast to Tent One. The primes to Dice's office, the rest of you have twenty for dinner," he called out.

With the AARI lamps shut down, the portable air conditioners came on, freezing the wilting snowmelt. The crew was in shock, some trying to puzzle out the abrupt change in script and storyline. They kept their thoughts to themselves, not daring to approach any of us primes with their namby-pamby, impotent questions and concerns.

Our lead writer was the only one to approach Dice. As always, she was super-glued to his hip and cock and ear. Those two goo-connected brains headed off for Dice's office in Tent Two. The AD and DP both looking pained by ulcers or constipation, trailed them, phones in one hand, script clipboards in the other.

I decided to give them two minutes. They needed to get their oh-so-witty and caustic dude talk out of their systems. Like the sad end of a grand ball or a well-oiled orgy, the three circles dissolved, the crews and cast moving off for food, drink, drugs, blowjobs, wet-finger diddling, gossip, panting, post-coital apologies, and Instagram posts.

The lead makeup artist kid, Steve something, approached me hesitantly, hand half raised, wanting to ask or tell me something. I'll give him this, the fake blood on his fingers looked real. I wagered an eighty-five percent chance he wanted a reshoot.

"See the AD," I cut him off before he got a word out.

Nodding like a toy monkey and eyes blinking fast, he braved a step closer. I have a talent, a reputation if you like, for making crew members disappear on return flights for doing as little as making creative suggestions, or worse, asking questions. His work on the back of Trenton's head was well done, so what could he want? I put my hand up, dismissing him, and walked away through the equipment bays, cameras, and support rigs. Stepping outside, I made my way alongside the service and equipment trucks, past the cast RVs and trailers, to Tent Two.

I say 'tent,' and you think camping, weenies on sticks and ghost stories. Try the Hollywood Roosevelt Hotel, a grand send-up under canvas. With five-star restaurant catering and a formal- dressed wait staff, the interior was an elegant swirl. At the center was a black leather couch, two loveseats, and a table, all warmed by tall, white candles. A tent, indeed.

Dice sat on the center couch with his pet writer, Bear, the DP, and Touch the AD, at his sides. If there was a fourth seat, I certainly deserved it, but there wasn't. I was ninety-seven percent certain this was by Dice's design. Weeks back, in preproduction at the studio, we had crossed swords. The issue? Money, of course. He was burning through it, insisting on the very best talent money could buy.

My counter? Camera operators, audio techs, and the like were just trained monkeys. You could say that lit his fuse. By the time we debarked for these second-unit shoots in this snow-covered shit hole of a town, nothing had changed. He had his ideal crew and I was left to cook the books.

There he sat with his inner circle looking like the leader of a circle jerk. The three men were sucking on their vapes like they were giving themselves blowjobs, spewing exotic-flavored smoke. The Pet abstained, surely saving her adorable, thin-lipped mouth for later. She was quite beautiful in a smart and intense way. My bet? It was her bubbled gymnast's rear that had kept her on Dice's radar for longer than two weeks.

While Dice held court, Bear was sketching on the script margins and his shot log. He was a tan cherub with darting laser eyes of inspired or drugged brilliance. Listening to Dice, he was also drawing fervently, working up new and creative camera angles, viewfinder compositions, and color pallets.

Touch was waiting for a pause in Dice's stream of nonsense for a chance to ask a question. Dice was all pale skin, black beard, black hair, black eyebrows, flashing his shark's grin while going on and on.

I didn't give a rat's ass about the drastic story change for this abortion of a sequel, but these three did. Pet, the writer, also didn't get a say. She was scratching a pencil on a legal pad like all good clerical help does.

Dice was finally taking up the subject the entire forty-seven members of the second unit were confused by, best capsulated earlier on set by Bear.

"What the dog fuck was that?" Dice repeated, eyes sparkling with childish delight. "Let me give you a glimpse."

Before he continued, Touch braved an interruption. He, alone, had a friendship of sorts with the director.

"That wasn't in the script or you're not sharing the revisions. Which is it? Going auteur on us? Sure, it's a B-funded hack of a film, but it's also putting nude blondes on our dinner tables. Please 'splain, Dice boy."

I liked this. Someone was actually yanking on the dog's leash.

Dice put on his Kemosabe inscrutable look, his I've-got-a-brilliant-and-daring-secret expression. Sucking deep on his vape, he blew out a swirling cloud of flavored smoke.

"I've changed the key, so tune up your instruments." Dice gave a daring grin.

I had heard enough of this and stepped closer, hand raised.

"Trenton's one of our three A Talents, a big part of the money on this," I said. "And you off him sixteen minutes in? Da fuck?"

Touch looked over to me, alarm in his eyes. "Wait. Are you saying that if Dice writes him out, we lose money?"

"Besides contract legalities, we'll take a 1.7 mil hit," I explained. "We're already in the hole before this terrible decision."

"What are the current numbers?" Dice asked, looking worried for once.

"I'm re-working those. This is a serious hit. Might be deadly," I answered, liking the way he blinked at that.

"Care fuck all for that. Where are you taking the film, Dice?" Bear asked, looking down at the two clipboards on his knees.

Instead of answering, Dice dragged out his pretentious Buddha smile and started whispering to his Pet.

The film we were supposed to be making was the sequel to *Rascals*. That one did very well, obscenely well, earning a 256% profit over production costs. *Rascals – The Sequel* had a much smaller budget, a third of the funding. Clearly, the studio execs had hedged their bets. Only three of the original stars—now two—had signed. Like the first movie, we were supposed to be telling the story of a gang of runts being clever, resourceful, bonding, and all that nonsense. By offing Trenton, we were losing a huge chunk of cash. Blowing off the back of his head erased one of the three profit-ensuring stars. Kudos, by the way, to special effects and makeup.

"It's in your hands," Dice finally spoke, looking at me.

"What is?" I asked.

"Go smooth Trenton's agent."

Perfect. Toss the grenade in my lap, you coward. I didn't say that, of course.

Leaving them to their babbling about the abrupt change in the storyline, I was already calculating my next round of magic money tricks. I headed for Tent One, ninety percent sure I would see the agent inside, still trying to steal and sign our six-year-old wunderkind star, the punk playing Frau Graves. Since the start of production, this greedy bitch had been doing her best to get her head far up the little girl's woo-hoo.

If Tent Two was the Hollywood Roosevelt, Tent One was the X-rated Bat Cave. Just inside the black curtain, I saw the two groups segregated as usual—the A-list and the Replace-ables. The *could-be* and *never-be* actors and actresses had the forward area of the tent. Their camp was a circle of second-hand couches and tables with gaming monitors. Three of them were sucking on bongs, the air over their heads a hazy cloud. To the left was an open bar and untouched buffet. They were still in costume and makeup, all facial scars and bruises untouched. Their filthy 1840s clothing was covered with stage blood and dirt stains.

Ignoring the Replaceables as they deserved, I waved through the smoke, heading for the bar. Fat Boy was perched on the border, sitting on a bar stool between the two groups. Beside him was the ass-licking agent staring into the A-list area, hoping and praying for a chance to talk to Frau Graves, to work her clawing, fawning magic. I leaned my back against the bar beside her.

"We need to talk through today's change. It won't take long," I said.

She ignored me, pretending to find Fat Boy's loud blabbering fascinating. He was trying to get the attention of the A-list gang.

"Best video game of the year?" he called to them. "Well, Monte, I'm gonna go with the hands-up crowd favorite. The ladies and gentlemen in the audience are united. This year's great First-Person Shooter is full of single-player explosions, endless milk-blasting levels, and filled with heart and hand-clenching action. Hundreds of levels to explore, each featuring a catalog of characters. In it you get to experience stepmoms and stepdads home at odd hours, MILFs, cougars, and savory Asians. It's *explosive. A repetitive hit. A splash.* The winner is PornHub."

He had both groups' attention, and laughter filled the tent. The agent was the only one not amused. Her chance to fondle Frau Graves with pen in hand was fading.

"Have a double Bombay Sapphire," I suggested to her, having seen her swill it before. I asked for a bottle of Veer water.

One of the Replaceables yelled across to Fat Boy, "You're higher than a grilled jellyfish."

"High as a fried lizard," another chimed.

"Butt puppet," he countered.

"Ass tramp."

"Vagina mite," Sarah Graves joined the fray.

"Cunt worm," Fat Boy shouted at her, laughing.

"Ass snake," another kid shouted.

"Ass slut," six-year-old Frau Graves kicked in.

Heads turned, she usually stayed out of these colorful and creative insult battles.

"Delightful," the agent sounded pained. Over the lip of her glass of gin and ice, she said the one word that could amp up my worries and stress.

"Trenton."

"Yes, that." In the back of my mind, I heard the brush of

coarse black fabric scrapping across stage boards. I did my best to shake it off and focus.

"He's going to get full pay and the same points," I offered.

"He's no further in than the first sixteen minutes."

I stall by taking a sip of Veen.

"Do we work this with legal? Maybe *you* can't," she drilled into my soft spot, the limitations of my reach and influence.

"*I* can work this. Give me twenty-four."

"You get twelve, then I'm running this up."

"I'll work my magic," I said with as much confidence as I could muster.

While she took a not-so-ladylike gulp, I scanned the antics in Tent Two, the two groups still divided but enjoying their verbal back and forth slugfest.

"When I'm an A," Fat Boy shouted, "Two-thirds of all teenagers are going to have my twanger in their mouths."

"Your mouth is a cum trench," Sarah Graves shouted back, sputtering with laughter.

A video game controller took flight. A bong arced across the smoky air in the opposite direction, smashing on a tent pole with a spray of glass.

"That was mine!"

"Nasty yanker!"

A tray of hors d'oeuvres took a Frisbee flight, and their version of a pillow fight erupted, a fierce battle of trench warfare. Food and cushions and ashtrays flew back and forth, the two armies hunkered behind the couches shouting insults and firing whatever their hands found.

"Here's some K-Y Jelly." I turned to the agent. "You want a one-on-one with her?" I pointed to Frau Graves ducking from a flying turkey leg. "Then we keep our Trenton thing downstairs. Deal?"

The hard-eyed, greedy alcoholic looked up at the tent

ceiling, lips twisted in thought. I watched her take another brain-numbing mouthful of Bombay.

The tent's canvas door opened and the special effects tech made a bee-line for the sodden agent. His eyes were red, his chin trembling, and his hands and arms were covered with makeup blood. He pressed his lips to her lacquered hair and ear and shouted over the din of the war in full stride.

I heard him easily, and as soon as he was done, I started calculating. There would be a nightmare of legalities and a PR horror show. More importantly, serious money was at risk. My private black curtain was trying to part again. Stress did that, not me.

"What?" the agent looked at the tech like he had sunk fangs in her neck.

"The armory tech is being questioned by security," he said, "Somehow, the gun was swapped."

He and the agent began their hand wringing, yelling back and forth. I left them to that, already looking for ways to spin the news as best as I could.

Trenton was dead. As in *career-ending* dead.

CHAPTER 5

The Price Is Right

*F*ollowing Trenton's death, production was shuttered for eleven days. The film set became a hornet's nest of police, studio suits, insurers, press, and lawyers. Back in Los Angeles, his funeral was a flashbulb carnival. I didn't attend, remaining on location where I was actually needed.

With the armory tech facing serious charges, accident or not, I was still able to bond him out. With that dealt with, I turned to meaningful problems.

My office was inside a Mercedes Plateau TS, an elegant mini RV. While a bit cramped, it afforded me the rare and exclusive status I deserved—a prime with private quarters. Not a roomy Airstream like Dice and his pet shared, but also far removed from the rented single-wide trailers the crew and Replaceables were in.

Inside my modern, platinum and silver office, I went to

work pulling the levers and twisting the dials of the production's finances. And my own. There's a magic to properly cooking the books, and I was one of the best—Flor, the numbers magician—with or without top hat and cape. This lower-budget sequel didn't have many areas to cut and slice, but I had my ways. Besides being low on funding, *Rascals – The Sequel* was low on plot and coherence, making it a perfect candidate for the studio's sausage grinder. This cinematic pablum might well pay off in international sales and instant placement in Netflix.

Working the phones, Skype, and email, I also worked the Pauline Place issue. She was our one adult A-list actress, who wouldn't get on a jet until I reconciled the bounced check. Actually, two bounced checks. I was on hold for a conference call with her agent and our accounting exec—another drug-addled CPA who also happened to be knock-out beautiful.

On my last film, I pulled off a big-time-money card trick and was confident I could do it again. But at that moment, I was knee-deep in the mud-filled trenches, playing hide and seek with millions and half millions, my head up the ass of every investor and financier. Everyone wants to be in the *business*, getting ringside treatment, attending meet-and-greets and movie set visits. I made sure all that happened as long they picked up their Monte Blanc pens and wrote the fucking checks. *Most* of the time, the funds cleared after a whirl of cocktails with a star. Talk about expensive hangovers.

While I waited for the conference call to start, I sent one of the pale and flaccid investors a not-so-subtle reminder to wire promised funding. If that didn't happen, my next step would be to crank up a veiled and wounding threat. A few unkind, embarrassing, and scripted remarks by a hurt and offended actress was often enough to get the money moving. On my three-monitor Mac, I closed my email and turned to the numbers—the real and the ones I'm reporting to the studio.

Someone knocked on the door. Why bother with manners and call me first? I got up and unlocked the door, and there was Dice's pet with the well-guarded revised script. I looked her up and down without a word or greeting and returned to my desk with the eleven pages. There were three scenes, seven camera changes and nine reshoots for facials. The eleven pages were still warm from her printer. That day's assigned script color was a subdued rose.

For some reason, she followed me to the desk, ending that mystery with, "Dice says you and I should have a relationship."

"Sorry, all booked up."

"You're Flor, the one and only, he says."

"No. Wrong. I'm Florentino Urbino."

"From South America, right? Which country?"

I ignored that. And her. I was looking at the cover page, seeing the film's title change for the first time, no longer interested in the rest of the eleven pages. I looked up with "This is bat guano nuts."

"Is that a mop on your desk?" she asked.

"Did the studio sign off on this?"

"Looks like a mop."

"You're in on this? What's your name?"

"Z.F. Glass. It's a pseudonym."

"So, we go with what? Zee? Glass? F?"

"Let's go with Glass."

"Okay, Glass, give me a clue. Does this change incur new expenses?"

"No idea. Dice is giving the new script to me on the cards." Meaning the crumbled index cards he scribbled on night and day.

"I'll read through for expenses."

"Is that a mop?" she asked, looking to the side of my desk.

"Fuck you, no, that's Darryl." I pointed to the Waterford candy dish. Darryl only gets the best dog food, premium Orijen.

"Is it alive?"

"No, I'm waiting for the delightful smells of putrefaction and rotting. He's asleep."

"The title change was my idea."

"Great. The film now includes cannibalism. Anything else before you leave?"

"Yes." She put her hand out and gave Darryl a pet.

Pleased with waking my dog, she left. Darryl got up on his little legs and stepped over the keyboard and climbed down into my lap.

I returned to my creative money skims and cooking, still on hold for the conference call about Pauline Place's errant payments. My personal accounts needed an infusion, which I worked through my banks in Bogotá. Smallish amounts, around two hundred thousand each, greased through faux invoicing and wired through two shells.

That done and *still* on hold, I swiveled to the right-hand monitor. I smiled for the first time since I last enjoyed a round of *The Price Is Right*.

These men and women prefer *connoisseurs*, not collectors. I think they're ghouls with twisted and black-hearted sick minds. No matter that, their wire transfers most always buzzed through instantly. These funds added to the coffers of the sequel as well as my personal finances.

Since the day before when I opened the bidding through the very black web, there were four offers of obscene amounts based on the Camera Three snippets I posted. I also had the takes from Camera One and Two. I recognize the shells the bids were coming through and deciphered their names, not that I cared. These twisted minds meant nothing to me except making me want to someday hire a contract killer to end their pathetic lives. At that moment, I was transfixed by their largesse. The high bid was 3.2 mil. The other three were right up there. I spent a couple of minutes reviewing my past transactions with these sick fucks, evaluating their prior levels of discretion. That done, I went with the second-place offer, 2.9 mil from a faked Transcuot, Inc. in Germany. Sending a gracious "Thank You, but regretfully..." email to the three losers, I sent the wiring instructions to the winner. Of the 2.9 mil, I would wash and launder a meager 0.4 for myself. The rest would help prop up this limp-dicked sequel.

As always, the planned infusion of cash into my private accounts splashed on my black curtain and weighed it down. I saw it in my mind, soaking wet on the stage boards.

The conference call started and just as quickly ended, Pauline Place's agent saying there was nothing to discuss until the monies were made good. I played nice-nice, promising to iron out the regretful and temporary problem.

The reply? Click.

After writing to congratulate the winner, I built a second email to him and attached the files of the footage I would send as soon as the money splashed into the account. It didn't take long. On the left side monitor, I watched the transfer appear after refreshing the bank screen.

A minute later, the studio and I are up 2.9 mil, meaning solvent. Well, approaching solvency. As for the *connoisseur* who certainly lived in a castle in some black forest, he had his sweaty paws on the exclusive, illegal, and gruesome footage from all three cameras of the brain-splattering death of Trenton.

CHAPTER 6

Cannibalism

I talked with Orosco, the former SeaBee and construction engineer on set. He was a bullet head with a well-groomed goatee and smart, mischievous eyes. We were meeting in front of the support trucks parked at the base of the new film location, the ass side of a ski resort in *Nowhere*, Michigan, the state chosen because of the reinstated film industry incentives.

We were talking snow blowers. Eleven of them for seven sets to be exact. The air at the back of the set was foul with the sounds of table saws and hissing of welding. Generators were also working hard thumping and spewing gray smoke.

"Tell me you didn't buy them," I asked.

"Course not. They're rentals. And I had to. Warm spell for January. Can't help that."

"What's your current overall burn?"

"Sixty percent."

I calculated 6.7 mil of the 11.3 mil production budget.

I winced but thanked him. I had a rare feeling for Orosco —admiration. He always hit his numbers, no matter what nonsense the primes ask him to construct and manage.

"We have the Meet and Cheat at nine," I reminded him.

Orosco winked at my wordplay.

"Full crew? Really? It's a waste. We've got trellis, terraces, and camera platforms to finish by the one o'clock shoot."

The conversation had nowhere else to go. I turned away and scanned the base of the steep mountain face with scattered pines—our next location. The thin snow was being blanketed by the blowers sending up sheets of white.

"Darryl's black-footed," Orosco said, raising his purring cell phone. "Part Indian?"

Confused, I looked down. So he was—all four paws black from the patch of fresh tar he was standing in. My otherwise white mop looked pleased with himself, tiny tail flicking, dumb eyes wide in his tilted little head.

Orosco was coddling and barking at his crew, sounding like everyone's favorite uncle. I scooped up Darryl, ruining my long winter camel coat. Kissing the top of his head, I tried to puzzle out the routes for the crews along the steep paths to the seven sets. I had no idea how they could move so many cameras and equipment, but they would. Orosco's team was the best to be had at this budget level. And unlike filmmaking, they were building something real.

Heading back through the trucks and crew and noise, I ran my numbers again, something I was then doing hourly. The overall budget was 98.6 mil. A lot of money, right? So long, you're wrong. Our burn was about where it should be, within seven percent, but we were on track for an overrun of 9.4 mil, and that didn't include the 'oh, by the ways' that always happen, *had to* happen in this business.

Giving Darryl another kiss, I whispered, "We've both

stepped in it on this one." My ice was thin. *Rascals* hauled in 256 mil and counting which made me a golden boy. Which meant fucking nada because our overrun on the sequel was also on me. Darryl and I were up past midnight the night before, playing *Move That Money!* Before we fell into bed, I was able to wire the Pauline Place monies—they were no longer accepting my checks.

After dropping Darryl off inside the Mercedes to ruin the leather upholstery, I entered the Land of Tents for the nine o'clock meeting of all crew and cast.

If Tent One said stylish and cool man-cave and Tent Two was the romper room from hell, then Tent Three, the largest, was a luxury theater. This was where studio execs, investors, and special guests were entertained, the only reason for its existence besides our occasional crew meetings. It was filled with comfortable cream leather couches instead of theater seating, all facing a stage and massive movie screen.

When I entered, the Replaceables and crews were in the back standing around the bar and jabbering. There were three kingly chairs on the stage with side tables and iced bottles of Veer water. I hoped one was for me.

Five of the Replaceables were playing a new round of the game stolen from the A-listers, the *Sal Sucks Show*. Six Fingers was speaking into the wet lip end of a cigar, using it as a microphone and interviewing Liar.

"So, when Trenton's useless brain sprayed your boots, what were you thinking?"

"Well, Sal, I can only lie. We've lost a great talent and good friend."

"But, your boots?"

"Yes, those. I'll never forgive him." Liar pasted on an expression of deep thought. "The brain splatter was an interesting career choice."

Swinging the cigar to her other side, Six Fingers held it

out. "Now to you, our rotund pufferfish, we're hearing you're stepping close to A-list status. Your thoughts?"

Fat Boy took the cigar, his round face a mask of pained, serious thought.

"Well, Sal, I've admired and followed his brilliant career, and while I don't recall his name, it's an honor to go forward with bits of him on my wardrobe."

"I couldn't have said it better myself." Six Fingers took the microphone back, slid it in and out of her small mouth with three slow sucks, the little fingers of her free hand pointing at the cigar. "The studio thanks you for your time."

Leaving them to their games, I counted the chairs on the stage again. There was still time for another to be added.

The house lights dimmed and rose twice before remaining low as the primes appeared on stage, each bathed by a diffused spotlight. Dice looked somehow both serious and pleased, as though two trains of thoughts were running on his tracks. Bear crossed and took a chair with his eyes never leaving the towering screen at his back. Touch waved out to the audience with one hand, the other tapping the call control button on his headset.

I should have also been up there. I was the one greasing the tracks and lubing the engine, keeping this out-of-control locomotive running.

All three sat without a word as the screen filled with falling snowflakes. Subdued music played—piano and violin, a minor key fugue. The gentle swaying snow dissolved, and Trenton appeared on screen, his once good-looking face in profile, followed by vignettes of his brave efforts aboard the *Desperation*. He looked powerfully handsome for his young age, focused and determined with a glint now and then of a self-satisfied smirk as he battled and rescued.

The outtakes ran for two minutes featuring scenes where he was at his best, even when off to the side of the action.

The last ended with a slow fade to a black sky of white shining stars.

The lights came up. The theater was silent. Dice stood and led the applause, looking back at the big screen. When the mournful music faded, he turned to the room.

"We lost one brilliant shining star, but we have so many left. Each of you, glimmering. Look around."

He paused as the forty-seven members of the film crew did as asked.

"Today, we honor Trenton and are inspired… to continue on with this vast and meaningful story."

Dice stopped for a moment with his head raised and eyes closed.

"We have some business to attend to. After that, we'll be sharing the rough cut of the canned sixteen minutes so each of you can experience what your skill and passions have given moviegoers all around the world. But first…"

The soundtrack started, the orchestra playing the film's raw and edgy theme song.

On the screen, the face of the first A-list actress appeared above her given name and "As Sarah Graves."

The same treatment was given to the six-year-old other star, "As Frau Graves."

There was a buzz of whispering in the theater.

"Where's Pauline Place?"

"Fuck her, where's Trenton?"

The film continued, running through the credits, the co-stars followed by the primes and crew leads. Instead of getting star treatment, Trenton's name didn't appear until the end of the opening credits. He was given a seven-second "In memory of…"

"Surprised, right? Should be," Dice said to muted, confused clapping.

"One of the magical puzzles of *Rascals* was the curious

and inspired lack of character names, a touch of much-admired impressionism. With this sequel, we're taking another brave new tack."

He paused again to befuddled silence.

"Can he cut Trenton just like that?" someone whispered to my right.

"Course he can. Long as they pay him off."

I winced and shook my head.

Dice continued. "The film is taking a daring new curve. Before we let you experience the first sixteen minutes, know this. Each of you is now part of an industry-changing movie, one that will surprise and inspire audiences around the planet. So, chin up. Tighten your focus. I give you the new vision, the daring and inspired change of title."

Dice returned to his chair as the theater went dark. Bear swiveled around, eyes to the screen. Touch was on his head-set, whispering, also turning.

The cinematic story of the escape from Puerto Mita aboard the *Desperation* played. It was the rough cut, unfinished, but enriched by the dramatic and tense soundtrack. The transitions were abrupt, to be expected—no stylized dissolves or fades yet applied.

The small gang of children made their way to the island and performed their stoic and desperate theft of the hot air balloon. Their many nights and days of the flight were condensed to a tight two minutes before the pace slowed for the crash of the gondola. In the fear-ridden light of the first campfire, the survivors sat in a circle, injured and trauma-tized, shivering and appearing half-crazed.

The last shots of the bear attack were not shared—the gruesome death of Trenton from the errant-aimed long gun in Sarah Graves' hands. There was a final fade to black, but instead of dissolving as well, the orchestra ramped up the theme song, and the first half of the title appeared—

Rascals Two

THE BLANK SPACE following it was noticed by all. Falling snow returned, slowly forming letters. When the second part of the title was complete, there was confusion, and the person beside me muttered, "What the fuck?"

The white lettering of the subtitle changed, filling in with blood red.

I stared. I was shocked. I was grinning. On the screen was either an inspired choice or a decision that would ruin any opportunity for future employment in the industry. Three bloody words, the last letter of the last word swelling before releasing a single drop of crimson.

The Donner *Party*.

CHAPTER 7

Revised Film Title: Rascals – The Donner *Party*
Production Day: Fourteen

ilver-dollar-sized snowflakes fell relentlessly for the rest of the night and all the next day. Under the white falling sky, Trenton's body was dragged uphill through knee-deep snow and placed inside the mouth of the snow tunnel he had dug to the crashed gondola. Eleven-year-old Sarah Graves used her freezing hands to collapse snow onto his body. She whispered to his final resting place, "I'm so sorry. My heart is heavy with remorse."

Six-year-old Frau Graves left the fire and kneeled before the fallen bear. Warm blood was still pumping from its chest, sending up a white swirl of smoke. She inserted her fingers into the bullet hole, feeling the red heat coat her nearly frozen skin. Looking back to the others crouching to the faint warmth of the faltering flames, she called, "What does bear taste like?"

James Reed, formerly Fat Boy, stepped past her, arms full of damp firewood pulled from the surrounding pines and oaks. Struggling with the load, he spoke to Frau Graves without turning.

"We'll need a knife or a saw."

Sarah Graves left the collapsed snow cave and returned to the fire, tear tracks frozen on her cheeks, trembling and teeth chattering. She pressed her face and knees and hands to the fire.

"We need to take stock and plan."

"Plan what? We're alone on the side of a snow-covered mountain," Kesenberg, formerly Liar, shook his head, his gaze lost and forlorn.

"Our survival. Our way to California."

James Reed placed a limb atop the flames, and they all watched it sizzle and sweat, creating smoke and little more.

"We need to assign duties and roles." He lowered his wide, young frame in the open space left by Frau Graves, who was still over by the bear. "We've enough wood for the night. I suggest we bed here close together and try to sleep."

"I miss Trenton," Wormy Girl spoke to the fire. "He was our light."

Outside the reach of the glow of the fire, Frau Graves lay down and embraced the bear, struggling to lift one of its man-sized arms. Lowering it over her prone body, she pressed herself to its chest for warmth. Sliding her legs in between the bear's with her coat soaking up its blood, she snuggled close and shut her eyes.

The sun was a round orb in the snow-filled sky, a cold haloed glow. James Reed stood up, bones aching, muscles stupid. After laying another branch on the fire, he moved on unsteady feet into the clearing between the fire and bear. He could see Frau Graves laying in the arms of the dead, angry bear and something else not seen before—a horizontal length of hand-rubbed fine wood with a snow roof. It was four feet long and a dozen feet beyond where Trenton was buried. The lacquered wood had a carved design across its length. Bewildered, he trudged through the snow to it. Sweeping off a shelf under the decorative pattern, he opened a hinged lid.

"A tinker tee," he called over his shoulder. He tapped a seven-note metallic melody on the aged yellow keys of the out-of-tune upright piano.

Heads raised halfheartedly from around the fire, looking across with exhausted curiosity. No one had the spirit or energy to comment.

James Reed closed the lid and stepped out farther in the dense snow along the path the bear had come from the night before. A broken wagon axle lay discarded against the bough of a pine tree. Ten yards farther, a wagon missing its spoked wheels lay abandoned, covered in snow, propped up on rocks. The beam used to jack it up was still in place.

"We're not the first along here," he called. "And now we're blessed with more wood to burn."

Sarah Graves raised her head, looking across. She climbed to her feet and started across, looking down the mountain and then forward, seeing for the first time how trees and thick brush had been chopped and cleared by former travelers. Braving a smile of hope, she saw other errant cast-off personal belongings poking from the snow to both sides. Kneeling beside slumbering Frau Graves, she stirred her shoulder, saying softly, "Wake, my love. We've a new hope and a new day."

The child stirred, growled, and nestled closer to the fur of the bloody chest and arm of the bear.

Sarah Graves joined James Reed, and the two dug out the discards of previous travelers, working together, deciding whether each find was for the fire or a shelter.

"Keep an eye out for tools," James Reed said. "A saw or

knives. Not likely left behind, but perhaps."

Slowly plodding, the two hefted and carried what they could to the angled clearing between the bear and the fire, forming two piles in the snow. Books and furniture were set closest to the fire. Rolls of fabric, bedding, and clothing were placed under the tree where Frau Graves was dragging all she had found. Sadly, but not surprising, they found no food stores at all. There were heirlooms, portraits, and abandoned musical instruments. About to head out to search farther, Frau Graves paused. Before her was a lady's hatbox. Opening it, she found a woman's formal top hat with a black veil. Underneath the hat was a black wool scarf. After wrapping her neck and ears with the length of fabric, she put on the black hat and lowered the veil.

Two hours later, all that could be found and carried had been moved to the camp. Time and again, Sarah Graves had asked the others to help. At first, no eyes rose to hers, but eventually, all were helping, the survivors working and struggling with grunts and groans. The one hold-out was the seven-year-old, one-legged sailor, Snyder, who watched their futile efforts with his chin on his knees before the fire. From time to time, he stood up and added a piece of wood to the fire.

It was James Reed who found a dead, stiff ox, one of its hoofs poking straight up from the snow farther up the trail. His hands no more than numb paws, he dug until the bony animal was revealed. The carcass was picked clean of meat, only bone and fur left behind.

He joined the others sitting in a circle around the fire. Laid out at their feet were the two pistols and the musket, four food sacks, and the firebox. They ate in weary silence, looking dejected, cold, and exhausted. Washing down salted perch with a mouthful of snow, Stanton spoke up.

"We should build a shelter."

"No, what we need to do is head down this cursed mountain," James Reed pushed back, his voice firm, resolved.

"Not through those drifts, they're three times as tall as I am," Frau Graves challenged.

Sarah Graves nodded, adding, "We wait out the storm, then climb to the west."

Heads turned and looked uphill. Above the snowdrifts was a towering granite bluff resembling a chiseled headstone.

"Climb that? Have you gone daft?" James Reed shook his head, dismissing her.

"Perhaps, but I think not. We don't climb it, but circle it," Sarah Graves replied.

"To what end? Why circle when we could make our way downhill?"

"California, that's why."

"Yes, that. Always that. Promises and dreams of land and fields of crops. We just climb that impossible gray face and waltz into your California and select which lands we favor."

"I'd like a grove of orange trees. I've read about them," Stanton raised her eyes.

"That's it, just wander down into the sunshine and pick your place," James Reed growled at her. "Do any of you know that the golden California is part of Mexico? A mere detail like that impossible climb."

"I've heard that detail is being solved. Negotiated," Sarah Graves said.

"Nice way of saying a war is brewing."

"I'd like a farm on a stream with a meadow, full of rabbit and deer," Stanton said to the fire and smoke.

"I'd like a nap." Frau Graves stood and returned to the stricken bear lying on its side.

A circling wind lay coin-size snowflakes on heads and brows. The flames leaned and lowered.

"I have the map." Sarah Graves looked for any eyes that would meet hers. "If our reckoning is right, we're on the wrong side of the Sierras, but close, perhaps seven to ten miles up and over and down into the Sacramento Valley."

"Where the Mexicans are merrily preparing our welcoming," James Reed soured the image.

"I've looked at her map," Kesenberg warbled in his tongueless voice, trying to sound helpful and also neutral, "We go east, and all we get is that endless salt lake, desert, and cruel heat."

"How long will our food last?" Stanton asked the fire. That question swirled in the icy air unanswered.

James Reed stood, taking up a length of rope. "I'm off for more wood. We've enough for now, but not much more."

"Where did you get that map?" Kesenberg asked Sarah Graves, his voice shivering, looking not to her eyes but her coat where she kept it stowed.

James Reed turned around. "Yes, your magical map. How did you come by it?"

"There was this woman we met on our way to Puerto Mita. She took us in and told us if we could make our way and join up, she'd give and honor land grants. All we have to do in exchange is pass the word to the wagon trains to turn south for California and avoid Oregon. She's written a book on it, including the details of a cut-off that will save the trains miles and days."

"So, our salvation comes from a book by a *woman*?" Kesenberg shook snow from his filthy hair. He was using a brain-size rock to chip a piece of flint into a knife edge. "I'm going to carve your sister's cozy bed so we can have steaks for dinner."

"What do we eat when we run out of bear?" James Reed was looking up the trail to the drifts past Trenton's boot heels poking from the snow.

No one spoke. Two members of the party got to their feet and left the warmth of the fire. Using lengths of coarse rope taken from the balloon gondola, they knotted the tops of the remaining food sacks. After tossing the ropes up and over high tree branches, they tugged the remaining supply sacks up out of reach of bears or whatever else might find their camp.

Snowy wind tore through the trees, the first taste of a storm front coming across the mountain face. Brushing icy flakes from her face, Sarah Graves looked first to the granite rock and then up the trail.

"When this lets up, we need to scout forward. Volunteers?"

"You need to be looking down the mountain. That's where we're heading," one-armed Margaret Reed grumbled through chipped and missing teeth.

"If we don't retreat, if we climb, we can start new lives in California."

The heavily falling snow was filling and blanketing the boot-kicked trails in the drifts.

A few were looking up the rise to the base of the perilous gray granite, but most eyes were aimed down the mountain. Either way was grim. If they retreated, it would be down through the dangerous ravine with twenty-foot drifts of hard, iced snow.

Looking defeated and not sure if she would be listened to if she spoke, Sarah Graves stood and tracked across to her sister, bringing along a roll of linen tablecloth. After unwinding a length, she held out to her.

"Slide some of this under your body," she said kindly. "Wrap the rest over and around yourself."

Frau Graves sat up, her coat crusted with the bear's freezing blood. Her small dirty hand lifted her black veil back over the top hat.

"They want to eat my bed," she pouted.

Fade to black

CHAPTER 8

Film Title: Rascals – The Donner *Party*
Production Day: Nineteen

A rifle cracked from far down the mountain, a snow-muffled report that nonetheless carried to the camp. It was the only sound of others during the past five days of no movement or decision on where the party should head; days spent keeping the fire lit and eating bear with a parceled small serving of hardtack from the grain sacks. Eyes opened wide around the fire, no one moving at first. It couldn't have come from Stanton, who had gone scouting in the opposite direction, last seen making her way in the direction of the granite mountain to scout for a possible way up.

"We're going to be rescued!" One-legged Snyder got up on his good foot and hobbled with his crutch in the direction of the gunshot. Others joined him, all yelling and screaming for help.

"This way!"

"Up here!"

"Hurry, please!"

Their voices were caught up in the snow and wind swirling the ravine below, their words dulled and misshapen twenty yards out. Keeping at it, they called for rescue and salvation until their voices were worn-out husks. They stood together, hip-deep in snow, ears cocked for any response. Over the next hour, there was nothing but the sound of the wind. Eventually, they returned to the fire one by one, each with his or her head down. Whoever fired the rifle would have to remain a mystery for the time being.

Snyder had been assigned to oversee the food and supplies' inventory as well as deflecting bribes and threats. The wood supply of tree limbs and branches and smashed furniture was secondary only to the food stores. Others were responsible for searching for wood as well as the maintenance of the fire. Manning the rifle night and day was rotated. Should another bear or wolves come near, the plan was to ward off the threat and take game.

Bickering had been dulled by the desperate cold and hunger. The party had gone through a little more than half of the greasy bear meat. There was no fear of spoilage with the ice and snow. All the sacked food was gone. They had carved and cooked the bear's legs, arms, and hindquarters as well as the intestines and organs. That morning, the skull had been cracked open, and the brain cooked on a spit of rusted steel.

Stanton returned toward evening of that fifth day, staggering back into camp, a vestige of solid white, stumbling and shaking with wild eyes and a massive hunger—her sack of bear cuttings and hardtack having run out two days before. Refusing to speak at first, she plopped her thinning body before the fire. Reaching her red and scarred six fingers out for warmth, she ate the few remaining bits of charred bear brain left warming on the rocks. Seeing the smoldering rib bones with blackened meat leaning on the rocks around the fire, she began eating them one at a time.

Snyder sat down beside Stanton, watching her consume more than a double daily share. Frowning, he didn't challenge her. The rifle lay across her lap. All the others were around the fire where the last of the furniture was burning, a pyramid formed by two chair backs. They watched on as Stanton filled her cheeks with twice the amount of meat anyone had been doled out over the past two days. One-armed Margret Reed brushed the snow from her face and hair and rubbed her shoulder as she glared at Stanton. Snyder looked on in growing offense at the amount Stanton was eating.

"What did you find? Is it possible?" he asked her.

Stanton swallowed and spoke through lips and teeth blackened by charred meat. "The climb is steep. And dangerous. The snow is deep and rocky, but there's a way across a perilous gorge a mile to the south of that granite nightmare."

"Well, then. That's good news. A relief." Sarah Graves looked to each set of eyes around the fire. Few met hers and no one spoke.

"Slow down, there," Snyder snapped at Stanton. Nearly all the ribs were gone.

"She's having her share from the *none* she had while she was bravely searching," Margret Reed bit at him.

"She's not looking unfed. No worse off than any of us," Snyder fired back.

"The trail?" Sarah Graves tried to diffuse the heated exchange.

Margret was having none of it. Pressing closer to Stanton, she reached back behind herself to the snow crust and took up another speared rough cut of meat and leaned it on the fire rocks so that the stringy frozen chunk could roast.

"She'll have more." She glared at Snyder, eyes hard and a touch wild.

"Pull that back. I'm in charge of our supplies," Snyder challenged, reaching past Stanton and knocking at the meat on the branch.

"He's right," Stanton attempted to intercede.

"I'll have no more of his miserly nonsense," James Reed challenged.

Margret placed the spit back into the flames and rose to her feet, a snarl disfiguring her face, raising her nostrils.

"She's been out there for days trying to save us all," she shouted. "You cowardly bean counter."

One-legged Snyder was up on his foot quickly, leaning on his crutch. Sarah Graves stood up fast as well, stepping across and taking his arm.

"Shriveled cock hound." James Reed also stood and stepped over, protecting Margret with his back.

It happened fast, an act of rage and madness. Snyder swung his crutch, the thick piece of pine striking a vicious blow to James Reed's face. His cheek and nose gashed, James Reed recoiled back but didn't fall, bellowing in pain through loosened teeth. He pulled a length of sharpened barrel steel from his belt and lunged, stabbing it into the center of Snyder's chest.

Snyder went down, crumbling as his one knee buckled, the piece of steel buried deep.

The fight was over within seconds, ending as quickly as it had started, amidst screams and yelling.

Kesenberg knelt beside Snyder's stricken body, taking his hands, looking into his shocked unblinking eyes. Seconds later, he whispered in disbelief.

"He's gone."

Stanton and Margret were fast to their feet, grabbing James Reed and bending his arm behind his back, the knife falling and sinking into the snow. Shouts and cries circled the fire. James Reed had his legs kicked out from underneath him. Stanton smashed her fist in his face. While the others kneeled around Snyder, James Reed was dragged kicking and yelling into the shadows.

Only Frau Graves remained seated, the bear pelt draping her six-year-old body. Her little fingers lowered the black veil from her top hat.

Snyder's body was dragged from camp and gently slid inside a burrow of snow a few feet to the side of where Trenton lay in his own grave. A prayer was offered by Sarah Graves, and the tunnel was collapsed down onto the second corpse. The funeral was brief, everyone needing to return to the warmth of the fire.

Back in the camp, the talk turned to what to do with James Reed.

"We should flog his back and hide," Wormy Girl suggested.

"Too generous," Kesenberg groused from his wounded mouth, his voice groping to form words. "My vote is for capital treatment."

"Perhaps we bind him and take him to California for trial and incarceration," Sarah Graves said.

"Says were heading that way like it's been decided," Wormy Girl bitterly complained.

"If we're to be tribunal and jury…" Stanton spoke into the embers and tendrils of smoke before her shoes, "… I vote for the wagon trail justice I've read about. He deserves banishment."

That brought on a spell of pondering, few ready to draw blood among their small group. Margret Reed broke the spell.

"Where's he to go? It's a certain death, a death sentence,"

her plea was emotional. "Don't think that would cleanse your hands."

"I say we put it to a vote," Sarah Graves' voice was firm, resolved.

Cold, trembling hands rose except for Frau Graves, who remained huddled in her pelt and veil.

An hour later, James Reed was allowed to construct a weave of limbs tied together with lengths of bearskin, building a crude pair of snowshoes. He was allotted two days' serving of meat. He was also gifted one of the revolvers. Margret Reed continued her pleas and accusations of heartless treatment, all to deaf ears. James Reed was granted a final night in camp, a dozen feet back from the fire. Sarah Graves told him to be gone by first light. Margret Reed huddled beside her brother, braving the cold. Neither found anything to say as the moon and stars were hidden by the passing dense clouds above. They sat side by side in each other's arms, teeth chattering, eyes closed, their last hours together passing slow.

In the weak, milky light of dawn, Sarah Graves looked up from the fire. With the rifle across her chest, she watched James Reed head out, his snowshoes digging tracks leading to the granite mountain painted black by shadow.

Fade to black

CHAPTER 9

Film Title: Rascals – The Donner *Party*
Production Day: Twenty-One

Two days later, Stanton volunteered to go out on a second search for help.

"If I can find that pass, I might find a settlement down on the other side," she told Sarah Graves. "Might be willing to stock me with supplies and send help back with me."

"Thank you, yes," Sarah Graves gave her permission. "You're so brave."

When Stanton headed out, she carried the second revolver for game and protection. She also had a pocket of coins from the others to pay for food and supplies and a pack burro if one could be had.

She left at dusk in her makeshift snowshoes, choosing that hour because the night had ice-crusted the snow, making travel a bit easier. She was encouraged by the parting of the storm clouds, providing a blue moonlight on the snow and rocks.

The others watched on from around the fire. It was their first day of starvation. Without a pan or pot to cook with, a section of bearskin was filled with snow and chopped bones were boiling, the fur burning and stinking. The previous day, Stanton and Sarah Graves had struggled to drag a ten-foot log up the hill. It now lay to the side of the fire, stripped clean. They had taken turns with chisel and hammer made of rocks, chipping off the bark and limbs.

Warmed by the fire, but growing delirious and stupid from hunger, the remaining children were bunched close to one another. No one offered to give Sarah Graves a spell from keeping watch with the rifle. Standing guard was by then meaningless to them all.

The sun rose the next morning into the icy blue sky, the first time the party had not been under gray or white clouds. The first spray of golden sunlight brought frigid winds that tormented the survivors, stinging and freezing their skin.

Sarah Graves had nodded off and the fire had died, leaving only embers. The others were asleep where they sat, each in fitful dreams or deadened silence. She bolted upright, the rifle spilling from her hands and clacking on the rocks at her feet.

"The fire!" she yelled, spinning around for of bit of wood.

The others awoke, joining the panic and searching for anything to revive the flames. Within minutes, a mound of sticks and bark was stacked on the embers. All of them fanned with their hands, shouting, begging, and encouraging the fire to restart.

Sarah Graves struck a match from the firebox and held it to the damp bark, leaves, and twigs, to no avail. Sleet was blowing across the camp, extinguishing her every try. The children fell to their knees, arms out, trying to add shelter.

Sarah Graves tried one match after another, having no success.

"That's the end," tongueless Kesenberg cried in his slippery voice. "It's time to head down the mountain." He was reviving the argument about their planned escape route.

"Enough of that talk." Sarah Graves opened her heavy, wet coat. Taking a piece of paper from inside the lining pocket, she frowned as she bunched it into a ball and pressed it under the leaves and twigs. Her trembling cold fingers cupped the flicker of the flame of a match and remained in place, protecting the hopeful restart of the fire. While the others leaned over the rocks, whispering and begging, she spoke to Kesenberg.

"We need to hold out until Stanton arrives with supplies. Then we climb. Climbing is our only salvation. Nothing but death in the salt lands awaits us down this mountain."

The others were too weary to take up a side and voice it, leaving the decision just beyond a stalemate, largely due to the force of Sarah Graves' voice and belief. With their heads lowered, each stared at her efforts with the fire, watching her encourage and patiently revive it, adding slight curves of bark and twigs. Within a few minutes, the fire was restored and growing, sending up a beautiful stinging smoke.

Frau Graves was gnawing and biting the inner skin of a length of bear pelt. The others took to doing the same, their teeth tearing into the dried, coarse stringy meat with long strands of fur in it.

By noon, no one had spoken another word. Each was busy chewing bear lining with sore and loose teeth and weakened bleeding gums. Their noses and ears and fingertips were in the middle stage of frostbite, deadened and discolored. The sky had turned an angry silver and heavy snow was falling again.

Frau Graves' voice rose vibrant with childish delight, startling all.

"I'm partial to braised steaks and taters." These were her first words in three days.

Her voice shook the others from their stupor. Half-opened eyes turned to her, along with weak, slack jaws.

Frau Graves continued speaking. "When we're in California, I'll pick a basket of oranges and sunflowers every morning."

Her veiled eyes were turned upward, not to heaven, but farther to the right, to the granite mountain face.

The others returned to biting at the pieces of bear hide in their hands. Sarah Graves stood and moved to the pile of their remaining supplies. Finding a length of stained canvas and two lengths of rope, she returned to the fire.

Snow continued to fall, blanketing their shoulders and heads. With the renewed fire under its canvas roof, there was coughing from the smoke but no complaints. Within the hour, all the children were caked with the relentless falling snow.

Their midday silence was shaken by the second crack of a rifle, sounding closer than the one days before. The distant shot was from somewhere down in the ravine. Sarah Graves raised her rifle and fired into the sky, sending a reply.

Minutes passed in silence. Only Frau Graves looked up from her meal, veil lowered, eyes to her sister. Sarah Graves squeezed her shoulder and spoke to the others. "Let's all hope whoever it is knows the best route to California."

"I'm going to go look." Wormy Girl stood up. Just as quickly, she sat down again, the icy wind shoving her, changing her mind.

As the last of the sun sank into the white treetops, a voice was heard yelling from the ravine.

"I found them!" A weary girl's voice, "Smoke don't lie."

The girl climbed another step through waist-deep snow using her long rifle for balance, barrel up. A few strides back, other children followed. A minute later, they stood at the top of the ravine.

Sarah Graves rose unsteady to her feet, rifle in hand, staring at the new arrivals. All of them wore raggedy clothing covered with snow, their faces wrapped in scarves.

"Who are you?" Sarah Graves called to them.

A white snow devil spun in the ten yards between them. No one replied. She waited as they worked their clacking snowshoes to her.

"Frances Donner," the girl answered after unwrapping her face. Her red eyes took in the fire before locking on Sarah Graves and the rifle in her hands.

"Have you brought relief?" Sarah Graves asked.

"Some. You are? What party?"

"Party? No, I'm Sarah Graves. We're stranded. Starving. We've sent a scout forward."

"How many mouths do you have?" Frances Donner asked, her eyes warily taking in the faces around the fire.

"Too many. One of us has gone up the mountain to find supplies and assistance."

The other new arrivals spread out to both sides of their leader, one step back.

"We're the Donner party," Francis Donner said. "May we talk at your fire?"

Sarah Graves looked them over, face to face, her expression hard.

"Our guide is a quarter-mile back. She'll be here shortly. The fire?" Francis Donner pleaded.

Sarah Graves turned around to her fellows. All of them were watching her closely.

"Yes, come."

Looking at Francis Donner and the others behind her, she

saw the same cold weariness. One lowered a full heavy sack to the snow and opened it with rag-wrapped hands. He offered her a chopped piece of pine. Sarah Graves accepted it quickly, greedily, and lay it across the withering fire as her crew scooted aside to make room for the new travelers.

When everyone was settled in and hunkered down, a second shoulder sack was opened and lengths of dried venison were doled out to trembling, grateful hands. No one spoke as the meat was sucked and made soft before it could be chewed with weakened teeth.

"You came to rescue us?" Kesenberg asked, his permanently damaged voice made worse by the meat in his mouth, a trail of juice flowing to his chin. He sucked it in and scanned the new faces.

"No," Frances Donner answered, unwrapping her hands and holding them dangerously close to the flames. "We're heading up for the cutoff to California. What little we have we'll share before we continue."

"This cutoff is around the gray tower rock?" Kesenberg asked.

"Is there relief *down* the mountain?" Margret Reed pressed Frances Donner.

"No, again. As you can see, we got here nearly as deprived as all of you. There's nothing to be had, no salvation back that way. My Uncle George and Tamzene have a shame of a camp by a frozen lake, but he's wounded. A terrible gashed hand. Tamzene refuses to leave him. There's nothing for you there. They face the same starvation we share."

Those around the fire fell silent, lost in disappointment as thick and relentless snow continued to shroud them.

"How did you come to be here?" Francis Donner broke the spell, "We haven't seen you anywhere along the train."

"It's a story too long to tell." Sarah Graves put a handful of snow into her mouth to wash down the deliciously tasty venison.

Another length of pine was set on the fire, sending up wonderful crackling sparks and heat. A second small serving of tanned deer meat was parceled out.

"Let me suggest a new story," a new voice spoke, strong and confident, coming from a few feet back of the fire.

"Who's that?" Margret Reed asked.

Sarah Graves stood up. The adult voice was familiar, proud, sure, and steady. Before her stood her one-time partner from long ago in the capital of Mexico, dressed in good boots and a heavy, warm, wolf pelt great coat. The woman's strikingly beautiful face had cold, green eyes. Vibrant red hair spilled from within the lining of her coat hood.

Sarah Graves noticed another child beside the woman and ignored him. She stepped from the fire and crossed to the woman.

"I see you followed the charts well," the woman said to her. "Landed on the wrong side of the range, but perfection wasn't asked of you. You've done well. Still holding the papers?"

"Yes, at great difficulty," Sarah Graves answered.

"Difficulty and *rewarding*. I think I'll title your story that way."

The two stood within reach, but there was no embrace, no hands extended.

"*¿Puedo calentarme?*" May I get warm? The boy at the woman's side asked.

"Yes, go ahead," she said, not turning her lovely eyes from Sarah Graves.

The youth trudged past, loaded down like a pack mule with heavy shoulder sacks.

"Who are you?" Margret Reed stood up and challenged the woman.

"My name is Hastings. Consider me your savior, leading all who are willing to sunshine and plenty."

Turning from Margret Reed and the others around the fire, Hastings locked her eyes on Sarah Graves.

"You have the twenty-three grants?"

"Twenty-two and a half," Sarah Graves opened her coat and took out one of the documents, showing her how its top half had been torn away for the fire.

"Good, child, well done. I believe that one can be made whole. Your fortune awaits as long as you complete *all* that you agreed to."

Turning to those circled around the fire, Hastings addressed those willing to raise their eyes, her voice strong.

"For each of you and your families to be, your reward is only a few miles on. Once you reach the golden land of promise and complete a few small tasks, each of you will be deeded land rich for crops and orchards. If you'll follow me, your future is secured. What do you say?"

Smiles were unavailable because of severe hunger, but some eyes rose and showed life.

"We can barely stand, and you ask us to climb?" Margret Reed swept snow from her hair. "And if we were to, what are those *few small tasks?*"

"Write a few letters." Hastings smiled. "Letters back to families, friends, to those back East. As many as you can to whoever you can. A minimum of twelve each. Letters of persuasion, telling them of the Hastings' cutoff, the new route to the promise of California."

"We somehow survive the climb and write a dozen letters, and we're granted good land?"

"Miss Graves here will post your letters at Sutter's Fort. In exchange, she'll grant each of you a six-hundred-acre parcel of the finest land, guaranteed to be along a riverbank."

More eyes looked up from the fire, taking in Hastings' confident and friendly expression. Not all of them were persuaded. Hastings saw that.

"Have I mentioned your resupply? Food, tools, warm clothing, and supplies? If you climb and take my cutoff, within two or three days, a pack team in my hire will join you from the other side. Each of you will be made right to complete the crossing."

"What's the surety of these promised lands?" Margret Reed locked her weary gaze on Hastings.

"Open your coat and show them," Hastings told Sarah Graves, her cool, beautiful eyes never leaving Margret Reed.

Sarah Graves winged the left side of her ragged coat open so all could see. In the lining pocket, the grant deeds had a gold seal of authenticity and guarantee.

"You've carried those all this time?" Margret Reed soured.

"Yes, I… it's always been the plan."

"And you never told us?" Margret Reed accused.

Hastings interrupted.

"Back in the halls of the Mexican government, Miss Graves and I partnered on this daring plan. At great risk, I should add. Now each of you can benefit from those brilliant efforts. All of the land grants are signed by President Mariano Paredes."

"May I see one?" Margret Reed stood up.

Hastings nodded approval and Margret Reed circled to Sarah Graves' open coat. As her nicked and dirty finger pinched a deed out and she started to read, Hastings spoke to the others.

"I'm off for now to ensure your resupply and persuade the other trains below to turn course and take the Hastings' shortcut."

"They're real." Margret Reed handed the document back.

Sarah Graves slid it inside the lining pocket and looked hard at Hastings.

"You nearly cost Frau and me our lives," she accused. "Other lives were destroyed by your wicked lies and greed. I warn you—"

"Gather your sad little puppies and climb." Hastings clenched the front of Sarah Graves coat, nails digging in deep.

"Hands off." Sarah Graves grabbed her arm and yanked the hand away. "We've been through the fires of hell because of you. Fail us, and I'll end your days."

"Calm yourself, gather your wits." Hastings dismissed her. Turning to the boy at her side, she barked, "*Señor Vásquez, de pie, nos vamos ahora.*" Mr. Vasquez, stand, we leave now.

Reluctantly and frightened, the boy obeyed. Adjusting the load on his shoulders, he turned from the others warming around the fire.

Hastings headed out, the youth in her tracks. Sarah Graves eyed them until they disappeared in the swirling snow. As they vanished, she returned to the others.

At the fire, Frau Graves nudged Francis Donner. They were the youngest of all, dwarfed by the older children. When Frau Graves spoke, her voice was made soft because of the lowered veil.

"I'm going to have a fine table. In a meadow of wheat and lavender with butter cakes and cream and pork chops."

Fade to black

CHAPTER 10

The Splattering

J was trying to work my voodoo with the numbers, but the phones kept ringing. Having shit-canned my assistant back in Los Angeles, I was forced to play telephone operator, taking my own calls. The latest bimbo had gotten curious, sticking her brand-new nose where it didn't belong.

She had clearly been snooping my email, getting a sniff of my sale of the Trenton death- scene footage. Surely peeing all over herself, she had sent me an oh-so-conflicted question. I fired off a message to H.R. about her faux-heroin use and worse, playing fast and loose with monies. Hello sidewalks, goodbye La-La career.

Earlier that morning, I'd taken a call from the studio's vice president of finance. Besides the overrun, he had threatening questions about irregularities. Stalling for time, I told him to email me the list, promising to resolve them fast. I decided to break the exclusive agreement for the Trenton splatter-fest footage. I had mountains of bills to pay. I began hawking the film to the other bottom-feeding bidders. And they were biting.

In forty-five minutes, I had an appointment with the A-list, Pauline Place, to ensure she was settled in. I needed to see that the production staff was fawning over her and handling any whim she dreamed up. Until then, I marinated and roasted the books—both sets of them—mine and the other for this underfunded nothing of a film, *a sequel* no less. With my brilliant efforts and slight of hands, the production was closing in to within 12.7 mil of solvency. My books, of course, were bubbling with joy. Even Darryl, the Blackfoot, was looking pleased—overfed and cozy on his back on the couch, paws peddling to doggy heaven while he slept. After three calls and more shell games with the production budget, I refilled Darryl's food bowl and closed shop.

Want to come along? Sure, you do. Millions of TV-tray feeders would die to see up the skirt of the movie business, slip up into the backside of the machine.

Kuddos to Pauline Place for arriving on time and traveling light, a tiny entourage of three. I had filled out her party with twenty-four-hour security and additional personal assistants. Early that morning, she came off the studio's Learjet with a sexy brunette aide, and for no reason I can fathom, a little girl holding both the women's hands. I was introduced to Sara and SeaBee Danser, both clearly impoverished by the look of their clothing.

Pauline Place was staying in the longest and most expensive RV parked on the backlot. The mandatory black brute in sunglasses blocked the door and looked to be freezing his wide ass off.

"Florentino Urbino, Executive Producer," I told the thug in shades.

While he fat-fingered his iPad, I expected him to be impressed by the 'Executive' I had recently added to my title. Unfortunately, he found my name on the approved list and cleared me to enter without groveling.

I opened the door and climbed up the steps. Pauline Place and Sara Danser were sharing the couch with script revisions and blue pencils, lost in oh-so-serious conversation, not noticing my arrival. I had to stand there like a lowly prince waiting for a wave forward to enter the queen's presence. I bid my time by studying each slight line of crow's feet stretching out from the star's admittedly beautiful green eyes.

I heard our other A-list wunderkind, Frau Graves, babbling kiddie talk from the rear of the massive RV. A second little girl's voice was joined with hers.

Pauline Place finally looked up to me like I had just appeared a second before.

Dice's pretentious auteur edict was that all the cast members be addressed in their role name, except for the golden Pauline Place. She alone received this rare treatment because of her many awards and money-making hits. She nodded to me, flashed her dazzling beautiful smile and went back to work with the other woman.

Frau Graves was laughing and chattering with the other suckerfish, SeaBee Danser, who Pauline Place had brought to the shoot.

Thing One and Thing Two came bounding up through the spacious hall, jabbering to each other and holding hands. Pauline stopped working her read for *them*, offering a sincere smile and kind, delighted eyes. "What are you two darlings up to?"

"Going for cherry-cherry ICEEs," Frau Graves informed her. "SeaBee's never had one."

Frau Graves was the taller of the two, not by much, and

maybe a year older than the fat one in yellow boots and red coat. Frau Graves was still in her filthy urchin costume and sunken eye makeup. They had swapped hats—Frau Graves was wearing a John Deere baseball cap and SeaBee's face was hidden by the black lace veil of the star's black top hat.

"First, kiss me both," Pauline asked the children.

Both little girls did so, happily.

"Let your minder know," I spoke for the first time to Frau Graves.

"She's right here, Mr. Flor," Frau Graves answered, looking from Pauline and Sara Danser, who raised her hand, giving permission. I decided right then and there that this other woman daring to markup script changes wasn't going on my payroll unless Pauline Place asked.

Frau Graves wiggled from Pauline's gentle embrace.

"I had sixteen babies," she told SeaBee in all seriousness.

"Where are they now?" SeaBee asked, equally sincere and with a nice, amateurish touch of the dramatic.

"I ate them."

"Crunch, crunch. Yummy babies."

"Enjoy your Slurpees." Pauline smiled. "Bring me one?"

"They're ICEEs, and yes, we will." Frau Graves and SeaBee bounced across the small foyer for the door.

"Tent One is cast, right? I think I'll go with them." Sara Danser set her binder and script pages aside.

The little girls jabbered from the RV, and she followed, *finally* leaving me alone with the star, who had an ear cocked to the happy voices coming through the door, a wistful smile playing as she took up the script and blue pencil.

I stood there watching her lost in thought, reading forward. When she paused to make a margin note, I coughed.

"Yes?" she asked, not looking up.

"Florentino, Flor, if you like. Executive Producer. I hope

you're settled in and the accommodations meet all your needs. If there's anything you need, desire—"

"Flor," she sampled my name. "The check bouncer, right? Thank you for making that right. We're good here."

She finished making the note and flipped the page over. Resting a notepad on her thigh, she scratched a few lines.

Her face, when turned to the cameras, had stolen and captivated millions of hearts and minds. While I admitted its power, I was impervious to its effect. I had to be, in this business. There was a rumor that when she was in her twenties, an audience testing said they would gladly pay top dollar to watch a two-hour film of her sitting on a park bench eating an orange, such was her beguiling and heart-breaking beauty. She would be playing Hastings in the film.

She lifted her pencil, read what she'd written, and pondered before adding a new line. Clearly, I wasn't pinging her radar, not being graced with her eyes or attention.

"If there's anything," I offered.

"You're still here? My apologies. We're fine."

I left, closing the door softy. I wanted to slam it, destroy her idyllic scribbling and self-absorption. I restrained myself and started for my smaller RV but turned and followed the music and laughter coming from Tent One.

Inside, the A-lists and Replaceables were in two claques, the younger ones over at the ICEE dispenser, and the older children huddled on couches around sodas and snacks before the video game big screens. Seeing no drugs or liquor on the table told me that the still photographers and video documentary teams were filming. Those behind-the-scenes snaps and vignettes were vital to studio marketing, so these chimpanzees with cameras are allowed most anywhere with my advance notification.

Frau Graves and SeaBee held bloody red cups with clear domes and fat straws. Both were sucking their way over to the buffet where meats and vegetables were being grilled to order. Fat Boy, oops, James Reed, followed them, once again trying to cross the border between the stars and oh-so-I-wish others. He offered to hold Frau Graves' cup so she could get a plate and silverware, placing his hand over hers around the cup. The other child, SeaBee, locked her hand on his wrist, saying, "You want to die like the babies?"

Taken aback, his fat face went red and his smile froze, eyeing the new girl alongside Frau Graves, who snarled at him. His grubby hand fell away.

I crossed the room, ignoring the older kids and their loud video-game mayhem. Standing beside our star, I watched her and the other girl studying the menu placard.

"Get in line, Flor," Fat Boy growled at me, eyes to the chef and waitress behind the serving counter.

Frau Graves and SeaBee were bantering and giggling to each other in private delight.

"Took me a week to eat my babies," SeaBee told Frau Graves with big-eyed seriousness. "They were big and cranky."

"Same here, plus I ran out of ketchup."

"Ketchup? *Eww*. I ate my babies with A.1. Sauce."

"Oh? Nice. When I have more babies, I'm having that. Crunch, crunch."

"Ooh-la-la."

Not making any headway with Frau Graves and unbelievably not hungry for once, Fat Boy walked away. I filled the gap at the girl's side. The chef wore a starched shirt and white mushroom hat. He addressed the two little girls like royalty, of course.

"What can I prepare for you ladies?"

The behind-the-scenes video crew was positioning itself so they had a clear shot of the star, capturing another glimpse behind the black curtain.

"Got any fat babies?" Frau Graves asked SeaBee, expression dead serious.

The waitress stepped around the chef with a deep pan of French fries in sizzling oil. I had the fortune to be stepping back for the camera crew when she tripped on her own feet. The pan struck the counter and splashed fries and splattering oil. Chest high and inches away, Frau Graves was struck by the spitting grease, taking it full force to her hands, neck, and oh-so-perfect face.

She fell back kicking, screaming, and waving her burning hands. Shrieking in shock and agony, she toppled over, the oil still burrowing, drilling deep into her skin. I shoved the other little girl hard out of the way. Hitting my knees beside Frau Graves, I watched her scream and flop like a broiled fish. There was screaming everywhere. Frau Graves was floundering in anguish under the hot camera lights, fiery orange holes eating into her hands, neck, and face. It was gruesome and terrible—ever watch money burn?

Within minutes, an emergency team rushed into the tent and the triage began. The documentary crew and the rest of us were shoved back to make room as medical liquids and soaked compresses were applied to Frau Graves. She was still screaming, ignoring their pleas to lay still. Her small body was electrified with pain, her feet kicking, her back rising and falling in spine-breaking thrusts.

Twenty minutes later, I had an urgent care copter on the ground. Dice and Frau Graves' minder climbed on board and they lifted off. I was untouched by this tragic accident but wore the appropriate mask until I was back inside my office. Seeing Darryl, I scooped him up and settled him in my lap at my desk. While not having a hand in Frau Graves' misfortune, I couldn't have dreamed and hoped for anything more. I was already calculating the windfall from the permanent damage to her face. In the blink of a spill, a star had been extinguished. My last sight of her was of baby teeth gnashing through the gooey hole in her cheek.

From my pockets, I took the memory chips and hard drives from the documentary crew's cameras and set them out. It was time to kick off a new round of *The Price is Right*. I composed the encrypted email to my list of morbid collectors. That got me thinking, a new plan revealing itself from behind my private black curtain.

If the studio audited the books because of the 'irregularities,' it was possible I might also end up on the sidewalks. If I were going to be tossed, no way was I going to land without my pockets full.

Trenton and Frau Graves' accidents had been personally lucrative. We still had A-list stars on board. With careful planning, there could be more misfortune. My black curtain parted all the way across the stage planks.

CHAPTER 11

Film Title: Rascals – The Donner *Party*
Production Day: Twenty-Four

*S*arah Graves led her party away from their smoldering fire and up into the unknown, Stanton somewhere forward in the wilderness, hopefully leaving markers. The going was exhaustingly slow. They made little more than a quarter-mile that first day, shoveling through the mountainous drifts of the relentless steep incline. She kept to the head of the group, sharing the shovel duty. Taking short panting breaks, she encouraged the others on in a weak but confident voice. Their path formed a tunnel with a roof of crusted snow. Three feet wide, it ran straight uphill except when coming up on boulders and tree trunks.

On a leaning flat rock under the branches of a hundred-foot pine, they stopped an hour before nightfall to build a new fire. Heavy snow was falling. With the others sitting in a shoulder-to-shoulder circle, Sarah Graves took charge of the remaining food supplies, doling out a single handful of hard-tack with a dusting of cooking flour. There was grumbling over the meager serving and talk of turning back, voices edged by cold and hunger.

"You didn't eat," Francis Donner said to Sarah Graves, speaking through chattering teeth, lips dusted with the sand-colored flour.

"I'll be fine, the promise carries me… carries all of us. No more talk of turning back. There's nothing to return to."

"You need your strength."

"The others need to eat more than I do. I believe our resupply will arrive soon. This storm will let up and we'll have spring sunshine."

Turning to the others, she went on.

"We just need to persist. I know you're all weary. Keep the golden promise in your hearts. Now sleep if you can. Let your dreams restore you."

The sky was milky white the next morning, the sun pale enough to look at directly, offering a faint and false suggestion of warmth. Sarah Graves stirred first, limbs stiff, muscles slack, her hands feeling like clubs as she stood. Taking up a shovel, she climbed into the uphill tunnel, leaving the others to the dying fire.

She dug for half an hour before Francis Donner joined her. Before them was a rock face to be circled. She turned to Francis Donner; the two of them squeezed close together by the walls and ceiling of white snow.

"Take a turn, please," Sarah Graves asked. "I think we'll come to a clearing soon."

"I will. But first…"

"Yes?"

"The youngest died. She's blue-faced and slumped over. Her hair caught on fire."

Sarah Graves turned from her and dug, working the

shovel hard. She didn't relent until the path had rounded the rock. Bent at the waist and panting, she looked to Francis Donner.

"We'll let her death inspire us on," she said. "We *will* climb out of this."

"Yes, of course, but we need to bury her."

"In the snow? To be exposed with the melt like the others? No more of that. We'll bring her along until we can bury her properly. A day or two at most."

The two went back to work, Francis Donner jabbing with a pick handle and Sarah Graves shoveling out the loose snow. Eventually, the others abandoned the fire and joined the effort, kicking and clawing the tunnel wider and ever forward.

Three hours later, Sarah Graves called for a break. By then, there were patches of soil appearing around the rocks and trees. While the others dropped where they stood, she went back to digging. She was encouraged when the ceiling collapsed on its own, blanketing her. Shoveling herself free, she continued, at times clawing with the freezing stubs of her hands.

"Don't you dare stop," she told herself. "The drift field has to end."

The ceiling caved in two more times as she dug farther, at times her shoes tripping on rocks and slipping on frozen soil. With the others joining the effort, the path snaked uphill, no more ice and snow roof overhead.

At dusk, the party had a small fire going against a granite boulder on a patch of dirt under a snow-covered tree. The dead child's body had been wrapped and brought forward and lay back away from their night's bivouac. Sarah Graves parceled out to each a handful of hardtack and flour, this time eating as well, a half serving. The others had scrounged enough firewood for a few hours of warmth. The sacks held no more than a day and a half of food.

Around the fire, most were too exhausted and hungry for talk. Scared and weary, sunken eyes stared into the flickering flames.

"If Hastings' supplies don't reach us by tomorrow, we'll be too weak to continue." Margret Reed broke the spell.

Sarah Graves raised her head from a stupor, shook it, and opened her eyes wide.

"They'll arrive. We'll eat well and continue. The snowfall has let up, and the trees are going to improve our pace."

"And if they don't arrive?"

"They *will* arrive. And our way will get easier."

"So you say."

"So I know. Now everyone, sleep. The worst is behind us."

At the end of their third day out, a camp was pitched at the base of a crevasse of rocks and crags. Too tired to attempt the climb and with the snowfall returning, the children lay the last of the firewood and branches on the hard dirt, kicked free of snow. Sarah Graves secured a worn and blackened piece of tablecloth to provide some cover for the fire.

The last of the food had been shared at noon, Sarah Graves refusing her share. Around the fire, all heads were down, coughing fits the only sound.

"What are we to do?" Margret Reed asked in a sad, weakened voice.

Too tired to raise her eyes, Sarah Graves tried to sharpen her thoughts before speaking. Wiping her face with a battered filthy hand, streaking her already smudge skin, she spoke into the worn fabric of her coat over her raised knees.

"Help will arrive. We were promised."

"We're starving. With no help, we'll all die on this mountain."

"We must hold out, hold on to the promise of better days soon."

"I've no more heart for promises. We must eat or perish."

Sarah Graves couldn't find any more words of encouragement.

"If, as you say, the young one died to inspire us," Margret Reed went on, hesitantly. "… let her also nourish our bellies."

While the suggestion was vague, for the first time since sunset, other eyes rose, some looking disturbed and disheartened, others showing a glimmer of hope. All were considering the gruesome and godless option.

Fade to black

CHAPTER 12

Nails and Hammer

*D*ice called "Cut" for a thirty-minute dinner break. It was three in the morning, the work clock having brushed past the seventeenth hour of the shoot. Energy and focus were frayed and the union boundaries had been crossed time and again in an effort to get things done instead of worrying about whose job it was.

"I'll move the fucking light tripod," Touch shouted, shouldering his way through the dazed lighting crew. While others straggled from the set to the dinner tent, he rolled the light rig over to where Dice wanted it placed.

Sarah Graves' minder pulled me aside.

"She's exhausted." Her nails dug into my arm. "I refuse to let her be filmed with bags under her eyes."

I pulled free, saying, "Plenty of drugs for that. You know who to see."

Leaving her, I turned to the other problem, another fish

to fry. A cell phone had rung on the set, a serious violation of the rules. It was in Touch's hands. He was crossing to Dice with fear and alarm in his eyes. I followed him, thinking, *what the hell's up?*

Touch handed the phone to Dice without a word. After reading the text twice, Dice shouted across the set.

"It's a wrap for the night."

There was faint applause from the few who hadn't yet left for dinner.

"Can I see?" I stepped to his side, needing to know what was so important to stop the night's filming.

Dice turned to me, his expression distasteful, like he was viewing an offensive insect. Instead of handing me the phone, he gave it back to Touch.

My bet? A ninety percent chance it was a marketing executive. With the tragic loss of the small actress starring as Frau Graves, the press had gone rabid. Their bloody red teeth were deep in our hide after the second accident. Along with the accusations of carelessness and worse, they were, of course, calling the film production cursed and haunted. Thank the stars above, at least the new title hadn't yet leaked out.

"What's going on?" I asked Touch.

"They're threatening to shut us down for a reassessment." He handed me the phone.

The message was from one of the sharks in the studio's legal pool. They should have gone through me. Dice had been ignoring them as usual. The tone was harsh. The threat was serious. A chill danced down my spine.

"I'll talk with them and turn this around," I said.

"I'll handle it." Dice shook his head. "Go work the new kid. I need her signed as in right fucking now."

Dismissed like an errand boy, I bristled while heading over to Tent Two.

I was no sooner inside when I was jammed up by one of the stage moms. This one looked like she was in stage four of mad cow disease. I linked her to Fat Boy as she started in on me. Why is it that these creatures think it's effective to attack while asking for favors? Having heard all of it before, I stepped around her, spotting my prey at the back of the tent. She followed, barking and mooing halfway way across before giving up.

Most of the cast had headed off to bed, but a few of the worst offenders were having themselves a time on the couches with drugs and video games, their minders having turned in.

Fat Boy spotted me. He looked lit up like a Walmart on meth.

"Yo, dog fucker," he called and whooped.

"Know what Flor's dick smells like?" Margret Reed joined in. "Alpo."

Ignoring the laughter those two had kicked off among the remaining Replaceables, I made a mental note to review their numbers and have a talk with casting. Their futures could be sink- holed with a few pen strokes.

Like a water snake in a kiddie pool, I tail swung over to SeaBee Danser and her mom. The child was sucking on a milkshake and flipping the pages of the white and orange book. I made out the title, *Go, Dog. Go!*

The mom said, "We're editing, care to join us?"

"Editing?"

"It's now *Die, Dog. Die!*" the little girl explained, taking a sip through her straw and interpreting.

I put on my interested face and even smiled.

"Do you like my scar?" SeaBee continued her revision.

"I don't like that scar."

"Good-bye."

"Good-bye."

She flipped the page and continued, "The dead dogs are all going around and around and around."

"You have such a vivid imagination," I complimented her, taking the chair across from their couch. At her side was the black veil the first Frau Graves had worn before her face was permanently ruined.

"Could you put that back on for a moment?" I asked.

She did so, lifting the veil so she could continue editing the book. She still wore the grungy and forlorn clothing from the shoot, her lower legs and hands filthy with makeup.

"You were a delight on set today," I said to her, before looking to the mom and adding, "Thank you for letting her stand in."

The mom, Sara Danser, stared at me like she knew something was up.

"Would you like to continue being Frau Graves?" I asked SeaBee.

"How would that work?" the mom asked. "The face, the voice."

"She'd have few lines. For the most part, she would be a silent but important presence. We can work our magic to make it a seamless transition."

"You could be a movie star," I said to the child, who had tuned me out, fingertip editing the book in her lap.

"What kind of money are we talking about?" Sara asked.

"Straight to it. Like that. Nothing like what the original was making, but think of the experience, the opportunities to travel and all."

"I need to discuss this with Pauline."

"Yes, of course. I can then set up a meeting." I smiled, hiding my quaking at the mention of Pauline Place.

The couch sagged to my left, and there was Dice, grinning, focused on SeaBee.

"You were brilliant and a natural. Thank you," he told the child.

"Momma? What are they talking about?" SeaBee looked to her.

"They want to drag you through the muck of long days and nights under blinding lights and boredom."

"And jump-start a promising career. A well-paid, life-changing opportunity," Dice cajoled.

I had this. The last thing I needed was the director muddying the waters. Next thing you knew, he'd start tossing out numbers like he had any sense of them.

"I'm pulling together a signing party," I told him. If he heard me, it didn't show.

He was smiling sincerely, enjoying the child, who continued to read, interpret, and murder one dog after another.

"If I may." I touched his arm. He looked at my hand like it belonged to an alien. That said, he relented.

"Gotta run." He stood, turning to me. "Be generous. She's a rarity."

I nodded, hoping he was done mucking about where he didn't belong.

"I'll join the talks if you like," he offered, which was only the worst thing possible.

After more fawning and sucking up to the mom and morbid little girl, I escaped to my RV.

When I entered my rolling home and office, Darryl was merrily humping one of my slippers across the tiles. No bouncy greeting for me, he was focused on his silk and fur-lined mate. I took to my desk, started up the PC, and looked at the blinking telephone.

Once again, I had saved the day. It was my creative pitch to Dice that had kept the wheels under the train by suggesting that SeaBee stand in for the veiled Frau Graves.

"All she has to do for now is look dismal and keep her head down." He had listened for once, as he should.

The first thing I did was read the latest online newspapers. The haunted movie-set stories were getting a lot of traction with breathless lies and innuendo citing false inside 'sources.' Rumors were also splashing with bold red headlines in the trades and online magazines. I weeded through all of it, identifying the slander and nonsense that marketing needed to either encourage or squash. We had one death and a hot oil career-ender and you'd think it was the end of the world for these hard-on journalists. Marketing would run metrics and send me trend data, but I already knew what they needed. While Marketing didn't report to me, I would still get my hand in the spins and slants. Go heavy on the 'inspired by the memories of' and have a mouthpiece give an exclusive interview describing our poignant tear fest, followed by our brave decision to continue making this vital and ground-breaking film.

I opened the four bids for the Frau Graves' Hot Cook Oil Accident and went straight to the highest offer. It was a cool 7.5 mil with the standard legalese about exclusive ownership followed by a request for wiring instructions. That amount almost closed the gap in the production overrun. I accepted the offer and transferred the footage and still photographs into a second encrypted message. I would send it right after the money arrived. The thought occurred to me—why was I busting my ass for the studio when I had my own pockets to line?

When the 7.5 mil landed in my bank on Bogotá a few minutes later, I decided to let it percolate a little interest while I reviewed my options. I heard black fabric sliding across the stage boards in my mind.

What would a collector pay for the pirated film of new deaths? Two or more of the stars in their final seconds before dying under the lights? My bet was a dizzying amount.

Taking out a pad of paper, I wrote fast and in detail. Twenty minutes later, I had the skeleton of a plan. There were still questions to be answered and an expanding list of things to do. Not satisfied, I worked on until I had completely fleshed it all out.

I sat back, satisfied. I could make it happen. And once done, I would not only have an over-the-top retirement fund but also an air-tight alibi. Pulling this off might also close the black curtain forever. Or open it all the way? Time would tell.

CHAPTER 13

Film Title: Rascals – The Donner *Party*
Production Day: Twenty-Five

The first meal of flesh was shared, only Sarah and Frau Graves refusing the skewered strips of thigh muscle roasted over the fire. Instead of eating, Sarah Graves stood under a tree, pulling down dead wood with a rope. Frau Graves had isolated herself farther, still seated before the fire but no longer speaking, even when prodded. She kept her head and veil down on her raised knees, keeping vigil on her approaching death by starvation.

Carving the leg of the dead blue girl who had perished days before was done after a group decision. This included an agreement that each take up the knife at least once. The cooking of the meat was made palatable by its smell from the fire, stirring the desperate appetites of the starving. Before anyone ate, Margret Reed offered a prayer for hope and forgiveness. The eating itself was a revolting fast chew and swallow along with cries of anguish and revulsion. A few of the children wiped away tears as their greasy little hands reached out for more.

Later in the night, the party was awakened by the clumsy clack of rocks being tripped over by boots. Stanton had returned from her forward trek for rescue. She dropped in front of the fire without a word, just a cloud of icy breath and shivering, extended hands. Seeing the stringy lengths of meat over the flames, she took one.

"You've been provisioned?" She took a bite. "Good. I've brought back little."

"You reached the settlement?" Sarah Graves whispered, eyes down, famished from not having eaten for days.

"No, I came upon rescuers climbing this way with pack mules. Sorry to say, they're undersupplied and struggling."

"So, word of our plight has reached Sutter's Fort?"

"Not that I know. The team coming this way is from a ranch in the low lands. James Reed was there. He organized the rescue before heading for the fort."

"Good news at last. I thought his banishment would turn him on us."

"So far, no. The meat, can I have some more?"

"After you know its source, you can decide."

"Its source?"

"There was a death two days ago. We voted."

Stanton searched the few faces that were raised. Dull, sunken eyes stared back along with blood-stained frowns. Realization came fast. She pulled her hand back. Entering the camp, she had seen a pair of shoes and legs lying in blood-soaked snow.

"No! It's ghastly. A sacrilege." She coughed up the meat and spat it out.

"We were starving to death," Margret Reed pleaded. "All of us about to die."

"There'll be hell to pay."

"Yes, we know."

"No more of it. I've brought food. Enough for all."

"Enough for how long?"

Pulling her shoulder pack forward, Stanton took out lengths of dried, brown venison and handed one to each. "I've also got salted fish and hard biscuit. Enough to weather the big storm if we're not greedy. I believe—"

"The storm?" Sarah Graves interrupted.

"Yes, it it's blowing this way, unloading tons of snow. That's why the rescue group on the other side is stranded."

Frau Graves whispered to her sister, not lifting the veil.

Sarah Graves leaned forward and looked to the boy holding Frau Graves' hands. His expression was as frozen as was his heart.

Fade to black

CHAPTER 14

A Million Tiny Holes

*T*he following days started with a full cast read-through in Tent Two, Glass, the Pet, handing out the secretly-held scripts and Dice leading the effort. All the black couches were pushed to the sides of the tent. He instructed the cast to sit on the floor around a large sterling bowl of fruit that was standing in for the campfire. Besides Dice and the writer, Bear the DP was present, crawling and viewing the cast through his handheld viewfinder and scribbling notes on his copy of the lines. The script supervisor, Alley, was also on the floor, binder in her lap, making detailed notes and not saying a word.

I wasn't invited, but I was there anyway, no matter the scowl Dice tossed me. I stayed off to the side where minders and coaches were studying the cast in pained silence. They had been warned to keep their lips zipped or find themselves tossed. I'll give Dice this, he was excellent at getting the good and rare out of his actors. He would describe the scene's pace, movements, and gestures and listen carefully to any thought or concern any of them had. When I was in his shoes four years ago, I had a much more effective style, namely, efficient autocracy. His caring and thoughtful approach made these overfed and pampered dimwits share their oh-so-important babble on how a line was spoken or how a gesture was made and timed. Looking engaged and receptive, he was demeaning himself and his position as director, crawling around on the floor among them for a reread of lines. Sometimes he closed his eyes to savor the change the cast was coming up with. With the children gathered around the fruit bowl, he listened intently like a pedophile Boy Scout pack leader at a wiener roast.

When Margret Reed reached for another imaginary piece of human meat cooking on the fire, the new Frau Graves, played by SeaBee Danser, ad-libbed, causing everyone to stop.

She growled the guttural voice of a stricken bobcat or like predator.

"Don't know where that's from, but please do it again during the shoot," Dice smiled to her, eyes kind and surprised.

"Nice touch," Sarah Graves complimented.

The little girl nodded, dipping and raising her black-veiled face. Edits were scribbled on the scripts.

Dice called for a five-minute smoke break as he stood and started sucking on his vape. The kids headed my way to the buffet and bar at my side.

"How's our favorite cum trench?" James Reed said to me, eyes on the pastries and iced chocolate milk.

"Cum trench?" I bristled, restraining my hands from going around his thick fat throat.

"Not you. Darryl."

I turn away before he died red-faced with a croissant shoved down his gullet, my hands squeezing.

"You're now on my list with casting," I threatened.

"Dice has my back." He shrugged, taking a bite of a cream-filled dessert.

"You have a slippery black heart," I told this A-list wannabe, not knowing where that came from, the words rising like my color.

His cheeks were packed and he was looking down, twisting the neck off a bottle of chocolate milk.

Planning to leave, I saw Margret Reed sucking on a bong like it was Dice's twanger. She was rambling through her lines to anyone who'd pause to watch and listen. In contrast, Sarah Graves was finger-reading her script, looking for insights, reflecting, and thinking.

"I've got eleven careless smiles," Tamzene Donner said to one of the Replaceables. She held a three-sided mirror in her hands, admiring the slight changes to her expression.

I stepped past, seeing Pauline Place enter the tent. There was no reason for her to be there since the day's script didn't have her in any of the scenes. She was in street clothes instead of costume, looking delighted and curious when she spotted Frau Graves. I had to be cautious around her—we were far, far away from being on good terms. The terms of the little girl's original contract had raised her hackles. I fixed it, of course, after an accusation of malfeasance. When challenged or threatened, Pauline Place had a history of flash-snapping from charming and curious to dangerously wicked and evil. I had experienced that in full color—felt her tongue lash, her teeth bared.

When she sat down on the floor beside Frau Graves. I slipped out of the tent and headed over to the set.

Orosco and his team had the snow blowers running, sending up flumes of white fired by hoses. They were behind the draped and insulated cameras, which were being serviced and placed. Long-arm booms mics extended over the set. Touch was scurrying around inside the set, deftly navigating the props, shouting back and forth with the grubby-looking audio and camera crews. Cables formed a snake nest all over the temporary set's wood flooring, slithering to and from the audio, lighting, and recording equipment on rolling rack carts.

Stepping into the rarified center ring of the shoot, I looked straight up and called out, "Orosco, I red-lined that."

"Know that, but Dice and DP demanded." He stepped to my side.

"And they offered to pay for it?"

"Of course not."

The sky over the set was a cross-work of aluminum scaffolding with a hundred-foot trolley rising straight up. They had ignored my veto of the zoom shot from high above, a ridiculously expensive and wasteful *artiste* touch for perhaps twenty-five seconds of footage. It was too late to cancel it, the money already burned. Looking at the camera rig ready to climb and film slowly downward, I was furious. I shoved my hands in my pockets to avoid putting them around any available neck.

Orosco left my side, chattering into his headset with other problems to be worked out. I remained at center stage, flushed with anger and something else, rare and glimmering. I was studying the tracks and catwalks above where lights and equipment and cables crisscrossed the sky. The catwalk inspired my imagination.

I saw how it could be done and received a deeply satisfying visual. The three A-list stars looking like Swiss cheese —a million tiny holes drilled through their bodies and faces.

Returning to my RV, I found Darryl enjoying *his* cum trench, my soggy slipper nuzzled in his paws on the couch. I took out pen and paper and started listing and sketching my ideas. I worked for three hours, ignoring the threatening phone calls and emails about the suspect financials.

When the plan was complete, I took one of the leased Land Rovers into town with the following list—get a local phone book, hit a library and steal the reference books, do the hobby store shopping.

It was an excellent start on a perfect plan. When I pulled it off, the black curtain would sweep open for all to see, slack-jawed in admiration and respect.

CHAPTER 15

Film Title: Rascals – The Donner *Party*
Production Day: Twenty-Six

The spiraling silent snow fell without a spell through the night and all the next day. The beautiful and graceful falling ice crystals were as deadly as starvation. Stanton felled two trees and with Sarah Graves' help, cleared its branches and sawed it into sections. Working in the freezing conditions, they dragged lengths of wood and limbs to the north side of the camp, across from where the remains of the two dead children lay.

The two constructed a small lean-to. With the fire having sunk from the heat, they built a new one atop a cross thatch of green wood and cuttings at the mouth of the cramped structure. Not large enough for all, the three weakest children were helped inside the dark and icy shelter, along with the remaining food and hand tools.

Holding on to each other in the darkness, one of the children was racked by coughing fits and delirium. The other two were too cold and hungry to offer help or encouragement. The harsh coughing and shouts of madness kept everyone else in camp unsettled through the night.

At dawn, the camp was buried by several feet of fresh snow, the canvas over the fire needing to be cleared, the fire smoke gathering, unable to fight its way upward through the constant downfall. Faint and cold sunlight lay across the lean-to's opening. The sickest child inside chattered a tangle of meaningless words before a final clogged cough. The following silence was the first through the night and the start of the day. The quiet was like the tolling of a church bell ringing out the news of another death.

Outside at the fire, Sarah Graves looked across the fire to Stanton, whose hat and head were pressed against her raised knees. She was snoring, her shoulders twitching. She turned to Frau Graves and put her hand on her arm and shook it softly.

"Will you help me move that body?" she asked.

Instead of answering with words, Frau Graves snarled through the lace of her black veil, her teeth bared, lips pulled back. It was the growl of menace and madness.

"Right. You remain here. I'll drag the corpse out with Stanton after she awakes."

Frau Graves' teeth remained clenched and showing just under the hem of the veil. Beside her, Margret Reed took a breath of the icy air and spoke with sadness and despair.

"We're stranded, trapped. Can't climb or retreat."

"Only until the storm lets up, yes," Sarah Graves offered, seeing the girl's desperation.

Frau Graves spoke her first words over the past few days. Her voice trembled, not from the freezing cold but in anger.

"Die, snow. Die."

"It will, my darling. We only need to hold on a little

longer." Sarah Graves placed a piece of wood on the flames. Waving her numb hand, she fanned oxygen to the embers, hoping for the bark to light.

"Hastings promised to relieve us," she spoke to the others around her.

The only response was from Stanton, who snored through her congested chest and throat.

"Don't speak again of your promises," Margret Reed raised her eyes and muttered. "I've no more heart for your nonsense."

An hour later, Sarah Graves and Stanton crawled inside the shelter and dragged the dead child outside, doing so as gently and respectfully as possible. The two others inside— ill, starving and dead-eyed—watched on, offering no assistance. Stanton shoveled a grave in the drift beside the two other dead children. She and Sarah Graves lay the dead boy inside without word or prayer. The falling snow would provide a casket lid.

Three days later with no relief, the food Stanton had packed in was a memory, the last of it eaten two days before. The camp was blanketed with snow and the only sign of life was the twirling smoke from the fire. Too weak to do little more than sleep in nightmare-laced fits, the children around the fire were silently starving to death.

Inside the lean-to, things were worse. While protected by the falling snow, none of the fire's warmth reached the three wedged together. One of the three called out, her voice a husk of its former self.

"Another…"

The Donner boy at her side had stopped trembling and died with his forehead on his raised knees.

Sarah Graves heard the girl's voice and raised her eyes. Staring dully at the lean-to's opening, she struggled to accept the news. Her party was dying off and there was nothing she could do about it.

Six-year-old Frau Graves rose on unsteady legs, pulling her coat tight before taking a tentative step from the fire for the doorway.

"I'll drag this one to the pantry," she stumbled forward.

Stanton raised her head and stared at her, her mouth twisted in revulsion at her words. Too weak to speak, she got to her feet to help.

Over the next hour, the two of them dug a new grave in the row of dead children and rolled the latest one into it.

"Return to the fire," Stanton told Frau Graves, who was staring down at the latest victim. Falling snow was masking his face.

"He should be next," she spoke softly. "He's still soft."

Stanton turned from her and crossed over to the fire where the axe lay against the rocks. She took it up and a few minutes later went to work.

By midday, she had dragged chopped limbs and branches to the back of the fire, where she hacked off the frozen green foliage. Inside the shelter and around the fire, the remaining children had taken to chewing on lengths of leather boot laces. There were strips of meat to be had, but each was braving starvation by avoiding it as long as possible.

They lost the fire twice that night, Sarah Graves restarting it with crumbled up land grants from inside her coat. She pushed the paper under the smoldering fire to the dying orange embers. At daybreak, she turned to Stanton, who sat to her left. One of the Donner Party members was between them, a boy of seven who had left the lean-to after his brother died inside.

"I need to borrow your snowshoes," she told Stanton.

"For?"

"Let's see if they fit my boots." She ignored her question.

With the snowshoes fitted and laced, she stood and looked up the mountain. At her back, tongueless Kesenberg was stroking a knife blade across a wet flat stone, sharpening the edge. It was his turn to cut strings of flesh for a meal.

"What are you planning?" Stanton asked her.

"Bettering our odds. Until Hastings arrives, I'm going to walk your tracks for that other group. If I can't find them, I'll head for that ranch. I'll bring back help and supplies."

"Look at you. Your legs are already unsteady."

"I'll be good. Strength will come to me once I'm moving."

"My tracks will certainly have filled."

"I'll find them. You mark any trees or rocks?"

"Yes. Two strokes side by side."

"Good. Smart. And thank you." She took a last look at the lowered heads around the fire. "The snow will stop. It has to."

She worked the snowshoes a few steps away, making some sense out of walking in them, her balance uncertain at first. Pausing alongside the *pantry* of the dead, she searched the snow entering the trees for her route. That's when she felt her arm taken.

Frau Graves was beside her.

"Take my skin," the child unwound the bear pelt from over her shoulder and handed it over.

"My darling one." Sarah Graves draped her head and shoulders and pulled her sister close. Frau Graves' eyes were raised to her, hidden behind the black veil.

"I'll go with, gladly," the little girl offered.

"Thank you, but no. That's very brave of you, as always. I need you to take care of the others until I return."

Frau Graves let go of her sister's arm and slid her grimy hand inside her coat pocket. When her hand reappeared, she held out a balled-up mash of hardtack and venison. "I spied it away."

Looking to the walnut-size press of food, Sarah Graves leaned in and kissed the top of Frau Graves' black hat.

"Go, see to the others," she said.

Turning away, she took one step, then another, clumsy, plodding, and determined.

As Frau Graves crossed back through the snow, she turned to where Kesenberg knelt before the recently dug grave.

"I can help." She took up the axe at the boy's side. "Perhaps an arm this time?"

Fade to white

CHAPTER 16

Black Velvet

*S*tanding between the wardrobe and the audio crew RVs, I looked up the hill to the snow blowers surrounding the set. Above it all stood the zoom-shot tower, high over the expanse of white trees, poised for its slow camera drop and pan to the cast's faces. The light diffuser panels up on the scaffold and catwalks were reflecting sunlight down from the clear sky.

I was headed for Dice's personal playpen, a ridiculously expensive, forty-four-foot black and gold Entegra RV. Originally leased, I had been forced to purchase it. Dice had Orosco's crew gut it and install racks of hard drives, editing equipment and large-screen computers. I had challenged this wasteful destruction. Dice's reply? I should have planned for this.

Losing that battle, I assigned the expense to the studio, not my production. There was push back, of course. Thousands of miles away in La-La, executives chewed arugula salads with blood oranges and sipped fine wine while sending me ugly threats.

I knocked on Dice's door, one quick rap. Not waiting for permission, I opened it and climbed the steps inside. What Dice and gang had done to the interior of the once elegant RV was an offense, a travesty. He'd had Orosco's guys and gals paint all the walls and surfaces a matte black. The former living room looked like the laboratory of a mad scientist, equipment and cables and glowing servers everywhere.

Dice, Touch, and Bear sat shoulder to shoulder all buddied up before three large monitors displaying footage, audio, and take choices. Only Touch looked my way, raising a hand to block the glare from the door. The other two were immersed in the editing.

"Dickwad, you weren't invited. Close that fucking door."

I did so, adding another offense to the list I kept under his name. He swiveled around, turning his back to me, joining the other two exploring terabytes of footage, sound effects, and camera choices.

On the couch behind them sat the composer, Alley the script supervisor, and Glass the Pet writer. These three secondary players were supporting the prime's editing of the last two days' shoots. With nowhere to sit and no one offering me their seat, I stood at the side of the couch.

I had sent the Pet three emails asking for the schedule of the zooming-tower shot. Three emails and not even one reply. I could barely wait for Dice to flame out on this current infatuation. I could see her afterward, sitting at a kitchen table in some dismal Midwestern apartment, writing the memoir of her one lost chance at acclaim and relevance. I could and would make that happen if she didn't give me what I needed. Hell, I would do it either way.

Failing to catch the eyes of that mousy beauty with her fist of colored pencils and open Moleskin, I looked to the three stooges. They were lost in the edits, highly caffeinated and whispering and pointing, creating cinematic magic with sharp eyes and minds and imagination. I knew better than to interrupt their spell, previously having my hat handed to me with biting snarks of dismissal. I nudged the script supervisor's raised foot, hard enough to uncross her legs. She was so lost in her binder and pens that I had to nudge her a second time. Alley looked up, one eye closed, the other glaring.

"I need a meet with you," I told her, hoping she would know when the zoom shot was scheduled and who would be featured underneath it.

This chesty young lovely would tell me, or her next employment would be as a fry cook in Ass Side, Idaho. She bobbed her head once and went back to interpreting Dice's over-the-shoulder directions.

Back inside my RV, Darryl was having a snooze with his worn out, damp girlfriend. From my desk, I took out the studio checkbook and pen. After calling forward for a Land Rover, I pocketed them and left with my folder holding the newspaper and the page torn from a phone book. I left the safe and colorful cocoon of the film location for the bland and washed-out real world. Having plotted my first stop in the Rover's GPS, I was sharp and confident, right up to when my cell phone purred. I saw a detective's face and number, both familiar from the investigation of Trenton's death.

I let the call roll to voicemail like his other three, but it had me thinking. The last call with him had ended with his request that I come to the station 'for a chat.'

The questioning around Trenton's death took me back to another round of 'chats' many years ago. I had been cuffed to a steel table in the back of a police station with a uniformed officer and detective. All sympathy and kindness had melted as soon as I was inside that concrete tomb. The topic was a friend's accident and I was on my own. My mother, as usual, not available.

My cautious verbal dance was met with their limp-dick taunts and accusations. I courageously and wisely avoided the baiting, showing masterful control for a junior high student. They had no idea who they were up against. After hours of questioning, they took me to the autopsy theater in the coroner's office.

The grisly corpse was undressed and exposed on a morgue slab, no draping of any kind. I knew they were trying to rattle me into a confession. Stacy's mangled body had been drained of blood, making the multiple injuries look all the worse. I looked her over, imagining her face and nakedness shrouded with a sheet of rich black velvet. That done, I regained my confidence. Those officers were up against the powerful mind of Florentino Urbino.

"We're still trying to contact your mom," the detective said. "Help us with your story."

My mother. When she was around the apartment, which wasn't often, that fist swinging, rabid man-hater had nothing but vicious words meant to stab deep into my young heart, railing at me in Spanish.

"*Tu corazón y tu pene marchitos.*" Your shriveled heart and penis.

She would go on, feeding her own fire in broken English. "Stay in school, weak boy, your way with *números* is your only hope, your only salvation."

Refusing to break and spill, I was taken back to the interview cell. I unplugged from the detective's threats and enticements, looking forward to the day I stood alongside another dead body—my mother's pale and blue-lipped, naked corpse. I even imagined how she would die—my hand pulling the lever of a machine that would plunge down onto her with a thousand long nails.

I was eventually released, shoved out through the front doors into the killing heat and sunlight. I walked the city streets back to the apartment, knowing I was untouchable.

Some days later, Mother still absent, the newspapers and school hall chatter were rife with mourning and weeping over the *accident*. I joined in, of course, miming grief and loss and sucking up all the sympathy I could. By the end of summer, the case hadn't been solved and turned cold. By then, I had turned to other endeavors, namely the design and construction of a spring-loaded board of nails mounted over mother's bed. I kept my black curtain drawn until opportunity knocked.

Shaking off the reverie, I drove the country roads on my second shopping spree. My first stop was at a local bank to cash a studio check for twenty thousand dollars. They flipped out a bit, but after the manager's nervous call to the studio, I was made good. My next stop was at a fabric store, followed by walking the aisles of Home Depot, pushing an orange cart with a one bad stuttering wheel. The stupid slapping wheel reminded me of my father's final departure, a real kick fest. Before leaving forever, he broke three of my ribs and dislocated my hip, going for my scrotum.

In his drunken stutter, he attacked with words.

"Niña D-d-d-dandy de un hijo." D-d-d-dandy little girl of a son.

I took a boot to the side of the head and out went the lights. That's when my trypophobia blossomed. Trypophobia, you ask? The adverse reaction to clusters of holes. In my case, a pattern of tiny holes set off disgust and panic. Over time, I came not to only accept the illness but also make use of it. There is a delirious satisfaction when inflicting them on others.

Driving along the sad excuse for pavement on the back roads, the GPS guided me through miles of unfenced fields of corn and other crops. The final part of my plan was out there, the mechanical voice on the dash saying I was two miles away.

I slowed down at a rusted mailbox fronting a dirt and gravel driveway. It led to a fenced-in wrecking yard with stacks of crushed automobiles.

A quarter-mile in, I passed through an endless graveyard of abandoned farm equipment, excavation trucks, and machinery. Just beyond was a three-story barn of worn, unpainted boards. Next to it was a battered farmhouse serving as the wrecking yard's office. I parked in front of the barn with its hand-painted sign—Roy's Demo and Hauling.

The place looked nothing like the fanciful advertisement in the phone book. A couple of men were eyeing me from a worktable just inside the gaping mouth of the barn—two bearded, gravy-fattened farmers. When I got out of the Land Rover, a third miscreant appeared, rubbing his blackened hands with an oily piece of dishcloth. This one walked toward me, twig thin, unshaven, uneven eyes, and a crow's beak for a nose. He was clearly Methican, a jittery stick ghost.

"Name's Roy. You the fellow called about a brick?" His eyes danced over me, the expensive Rover, and my city clothing.

"Yes, but what I need is a half."

"A whole one or nothing. Cash, of course."

"Will you cut it for me?"

"If your cash is green."

One of Roy's butt stains called over, "He good for it?"

"Seems so," the twitchy skeleton called over his shoulder, rubbing his acne-crusted chin. "Seven thousand," he said to me.

"I can go elsewhere." It was a gambit. I caught a whiff of a putrid fertilizer in the crossing wind.

"No, you can't. Not within a hundred miles." His breath was dank with stale beer and cheap tobacco.

I turned my back on him, knowing it would ring his bell, and walked to the Rover. Opening the passenger door, I counted out six thousand in fifties.

"Here's six. It's all I have. Worn fifties. Easy to pass."

He looked at the cash in my hand like he was still thinking it over. He took it, of course, grousing.

"You cut it yourself, city punk. Got cow shit on your wingtips. Hope it ruins your fancy four-by."

Tough talk. I didn't bother looking down. I could smell the truth. He went inside the barn, returning a few minutes later with the brick. I had him set it on the passenger seat of the Land Rover.

After he tremble-walked back to the barn, I sat on the driver's seat and took off my shoes and dropped them in the muck. I drove away pleased with myself, the key ingredient at my side.

CHAPTER 17

Film Title: Rascals – The Donner *Party*
Production Day: Twenty-Eight

Sarah Graves fell to her knees, facing the next hostile obstacle. After a minute of staring, her thoughts disjointed, her ribs and belly aching with hunger, she sat back on the steep incline in a tangle of tree limbs and uncaring cold rocks.

Unlacing her snowshoes and holding them in numb-cold hands, she stepped to the fallen log caked with snow. Using one of the snowshoes as a shovel, she cracked the crust and cleared the snow until the dark redwood bark showed. She climbed onto it, her arms quaking with weakness.

"God, give me heart." She breathed, straddling the log, looking farther up the incline. Squinting and scanning, she looked for any suggestion of Stanton's tear-shaped prints in the snow. The last few she had seen hours before had been mere hints filled with fresh snowfall. Seeing none, she worked her leg over and dropped, her knees giving as she sank, her elbow smacking a hidden rock, sending out stabbing glints of pain in her dulled mind and nerves.

Ignoring the pain, she laced the snowshoe on and continued. Ten yards out, she stopped and removed them again. The climb through the rocks before her was too steep and narrow for their use. She shook her head, uncertain if this was the correct direction. Her chapped lips clenched, she faced her next life or death choice. Get it wrong and she saw herself perishing, never to be found, leaning against a rock or tree.

"Get it right," she emboldened herself. "No more useless questioning."

She started up a rock-strewn crevasse, climbing rock by rock, foothold after foothold.

At the top, she paused, looking down the twenty-five yards of the steep climb. Turning away, she saw an 'H' chopped into the meat of a tree. The day before, she had passed Stanton's last double lines etched on a stone. She whispered a single word, shaking her head.

"Hastings."

Anger flamed in her heart and mind.

"This is your cutoff, your shortcut? Wagons and oxen are going to attempt this?" Disgust replaced the desire to murder the woman if she ever met her.

With that, she turned away to the next climb. Lacing the snowshoes back onto her boots, she worked up the steep hill through hip-deep snow, the shoes clacking and hidden.

The going was an endless uphill struggle, one step at a time, grasping for handholds that didn't exist. She climbed with her head down and teeth clenched. At times, winds buffeted her, trying to knock her aside.

Hours later, she stopped beside an exposed boulder. Raising her eyes, she made out an exposed level a dozen yards away. Climbing to it, she was challenged by ruthless, icy wind. The snow was then shallow, knee-deep. Pushing through brush stiff with ice, she reached the edge of the flat clearing.

On the other end was an impassible rock face. To the left, the east side of the mountain fell to the valley far below. To her right, a gorge snaked uphill, filled with rocks.

Removing the snowshoes again, she laced them together and shouldered them and began the next climb. She moved rock to rock, their tops slick with ice. A third of the way up, her hands and knees were nicked and cut, screaming at her to stop. Refusing to listen, she pulled herself up a few feet more and continued. Time and again, the winds smashed her against the rocks, attempting to loosen her grip. She waited until the gust relented, holding on tight. As soon as they had passed, she searched out the next handhold and made for it.

"Hastings," she cursed, laying on the rocks at the top of the gorge.

The desire to kill her was the only heat available. She fanned it, needing the warmth.

Rolling onto her side, she stared at the next challenge, a snowfield rising uphill marked by dead trees like skeletal sentries. Tying on the snowshoes with frozen fingers, she got to her feet.

Three strides out, she was chest high in white, uncaring snow. Kicking and digging with her hands, she carved forward. The snow grew deeper, the walls of the path falling in on her, blanketing the bear pelt shrouding her head and shoulders. She stopped twice, panting, feeling faint, blinking unfocused eyes to gather together her fleeting, random thoughts.

Daylight was a white haze overhead. The fading light was threatening. Unable to move any faster, she pressed on, needing to find any kind of shelter from the night.

Kicking the clumsy shoes, clawing and punching the snow, she gained five feet and then five more.

Two hours later, she was across the field, pulling herself up onto a rounded rock at the base of her next climb. Removing the snowshoes, she studied the way ahead. The incline was so steep that possible handholds showed through the shallow snow.

Two-thirds up, the angle grew perilous. She stopped with her chin and neck pressing a rough stone, her knees locked, her boot tips on uncertain perch.

Sweeping her hand upward back and forth, her fingertips searched desperately for anything solid to grasp. Brushing the edge of a rock, she clenched it. Pulling herself up, the rock under her left boot gave.

"No!" she yelled, trying to throw her weight to her other foot, hands seeking desperately. Her chin cracked on a rock, her teeth digging a bloody trench in her tongue. She slid and banged ten feet down before locking her arm around an exposed tree root. Her boots pedaled, trying for any purchase. Eyes squeezed tight, she focused on her boot toes, ignored the blood filling her mouth. Her right boot struck a crag and she pressed onto it.

Stopping all other movement, she tested the strength of the hold. When there was no give, she opened her eyes and looked for a handhold above, making out the ones used before the fall. Pulling herself upward, she blocked her mind from everything except the next rock she needed to grasp. Then the one after that.

With sunset closing in, she stood on the edge of a second clearing, a rock field no more than ten yards wide and long. The ground was blessedly level, and she paused, taking a brief reprieve leaning against the base of a tall, cold rock. Taking out the ball of meal and meat that Frau Graves had given her, hunger clawed up through her dull and deadened mind. She took a tiny bite, her tongue still painfully tender, after deciding to allow herself three. Chewing, savoring the bland hardtack and the wonderful meat, she looked across the rocks before her. Collecting every crumb than tumbled from her cracked and bloodied lips, she stared, unblinking, before clenching her eyes tight. She could still see it. Stanton's mark on a head-high boulder.

"Thank you." She swallowed her first bite of food in two days. The dreadful fears left her. Pocketing what remained of the small ball of food, she started across. The other side of the field offered a single path, a faint pattern of rocks forming the start of a traverse.

Half an hour later, she came to a ridge across the face of the unforgiving and relentless mountain. The sun was setting and the winds were freezing when she stopped for the night. Pressing herself between two coarse rocks, she drew her knees in and pulled the bear pelt over her chest and legs, facing the night alone with the frigid winds on the face of the mountain.

Her sleep was haunted, sometimes deadened, other times shaken by fits of frightened and threatening dreams. Waking from one, she pulled the bearskin from her face and took a breath of icy air. Shivering, her muscles firing off and on in bursts of dulled electricity, she looked up. The sky was an expanse of black with hundreds of glittering stars. Unmoved by the beauty of the view, her burrowed freezing mind searched for any reason for hope. It came to her slowly.

"The snows have stopped." She closed her eyes and lowered her head.

Dawn delivered a peerless blue sky over the mountains and hills below. Stiff, sore, and all renewed strength from the bites of food gone, she stared at the absence of storm clouds.

"There's that," she tried to encourage herself. It wasn't enough.

Her body was fighting her, insisting she draw her limbs in, curl up into a ball and put her head down. A black shroud began to lay across her thoughts, offering eternal silence and endless comfort. She knew she needed to fight it but had no weapon to defend herself.

It was her still-beating heart that saved her. That and a memory. Faces around a dying fire. Her sister. The others. Their last hope was resting in her.

Climbing from the slight opening between the rocks, she stood slowly, testing her weak legs and knees. Draping her head and back with the pelt, she started out again.

The day remained clear. Occasionally, sunlight touched her face with faint splashes of warmth. The going was difficult, but the pitch nowhere as steep as the day before. By midmorning, she saw that the climb was possibly nearing the mountaintop. The winds were cruel and unforgiving.

She stopped to rest one time that day, taking twenty minutes for a bite from the ball of food.

Sunset found her in a barren rock field with a strand of wind-striped pines up ahead. She stumbled her way to them.

"Too worn to continue." She found a tight space between a fallen tree and rock. Wedging herself inside as far as possible, she kept her eyes to a second distant cluster of trees.

"Tomorrow." She coughed, making a promise.

Darkness lowered over her like an unforgiving blanket of freezing black. Stars were starting to appear to the east. She was lowering her eyes from them when she saw something new. Her heart quickened and she stared in hope and disbelief. In a gathering of pines a mile off, a lantern light swung and disappeared. It had been faint, a swaying of amber. Refusing all doubts, she stared across the distance for a second glimpse of the flickering light. She would stay awake all night if need be.

At the first hint of daylight, she started across, trudging

on weak, shaking legs. Stumbling and falling, she didn't slow down. The cluster of trees was on the brow of a declining westward ridge.

Reaching them, she allowed her knees to buckle. She kneeled at the edge of a makeshift camp, nothing more than a dead circle of rocks and hacked tree limbs. There was no one to be seen.

"Oh," she whispered. "Thank you."

The camp was abandoned but provisioned. An oxen pack rested against a tree across from her. Two supply sacks hung from the branches above. It took her less than a minute to figure out the knots to the ropes.

The first sack held blankets and tools. The second contained flour sacks of dried meat and grain and bricks of hardtack. She built a tent with a length of horse blanket draped over a rope between two trees. Inside, she held the firebox she had discovered.

"Light a fire," she told herself, knowing she should be gathering wood. Instead, she drew her knees up and covered them, taking a large greedy bite of dried meat. She ate without pause, even when her gut clenched and twisted.

When she could finally eat no more, her shrunken belly resisting, she looked out across the camp, spotting a few dead branches. Building a fire was critical. And it would get built and lit. But it had to wait until later in the day.

"Sleep. Blessed sleep," Sarah Graves whispered and toppled onto her side.

Fade to black

CHAPTER 18

A Holey Mess

*B*efore I entered the Walmart, I removed my socks and pushed them inside an overflowing garbage can next to the sliding glass doors. It seemed apropos to go in barefoot, it being a Walmart, no matter the weather. I was equally sure my cow-shit-covered wingtips would have been welcomed as well by the retardo offering shopping carts.

Dios mío, the lighting, not a shadow in sight, a revolting nightmare, perfect for accenting the bold-colored products in blasting primary colors. There were miles of fluorescents reaching out forever. I was in a low-rent superstore as large as an airplane hangar.

There's no need for me to comment on the customers and employees there. Do yourself a YouTube search if you have the stomach for it. I wheeled my shopping cart through Sporting Goods and found what I needed, jumbo size. Next was Housewares for a dozen tubes of Superglue. In Hardware, I found a 'Round the House' tool kit—fifty-one *nifty* tools for $29.97.

I paid with cash, which, of course, caused stumbling confusion. The butterball behind the counter had to engage her brain to calculate the change. Far too many minutes later, I was out of there.

The GPS guided me back inside the safe, warm belly of the movie set. Turning in the Land Rover, I breathed deep. The air, as expected, was cleaner, rarified, and electric with the magic of movie-making.

Inside my RV, I carried the shopping bags to the back bedroom. It was clear Darryl and his missus had had a spat. He was alone on my side of the bed, bicycling through a dream with impotent growls and snapping little teeth.

After unpacking the shopping bags, I decided a cutting board from the kitchenette would work well. I went and pulled it out of its slot and took it and the stolen library books back to my bed top laboratory. Wanting to begin building, the incessant ringing of my phone drew me to my desk.

Seeing the blinking display from several voicemails, I thumbed through the numbers. The detective's messages were marked urgent, of course. Before returning his call, I thought back through the events up to and following Trenton's brain launch, draping each likely question with the black lace of planned words and fact-play and explanations. With the table set, I hit Return Call.

He picked up on the third ring, sounding gruff and irritated.

"Detective Barnes, who's calling?"

"Florentino Urbino returning your call," I left the bedroom.

"You mean my *calls*. I asked you to come to the station. Any reason why you haven't? This is a serious crime."

"Crime? You mean accident."

"That hasn't been decided. New information has come to light."

"Such as?"

"I'll do the questioning. I've been looking into the boy's past. That and this whole movie thing you're part of. I spoke to your boss in Los Angeles. In case you haven't heard, he's thinking about pulling you out. Have you been playing fast and loose with the money?"

"No, of course not. My books are pristine," I turned on my computer and opened the accounting software. Soon as this call was over, I would do another rinse.

"I've also learned that you're a co-beneficiary on Trenton's life insurance policy," he went on. "Care to explain that?"

Damn. I thought I had shelled that well. He was good.

"Standard operating practice," I said, trying to sound calm and collected, bored even. "The secondary holding company writes those."

"You mean *your* holding company."

"It's nominally mine, yes. In case of an accident such as this, those monies go directly to the family as a bridge until the full insurance payout."

"I've talked to the boy's parents. They haven't seen a dime."

"There's been an accounting hiccup," I lied again, smooth and convincing. "The wire transfer is scheduled for later today."

"Mr. Urbino, I think you're dancing around the truth. If you're unwilling to come to the station, I'm going to send an officer to come get you."

"No need. Let me contact my lawyer, and I'll head over."

"You're lawyering up?"

I heard a crack in his façade.

"Of course, I am. I don't care for your accusations. I find this offensive."

"No one's accused you of anything."

"Will tomorrow work? I need to fly her in."

"That'll be fine."

We agreed to meet at four thirty and ended the call. I could buy a few more days by blaming my attorney's busy schedule, not that I planned to call her.

That accomplished, going smoother than shit through a goose, I decided to work my desk awhile longer. By massaging financial accounts, I added another layer of misdirection to the books. Next up were the urgent emails from the studio. I skim-read each. So far, they were peeing all over themselves and firing off vague threats, but I was still gainfully employed. That's all I needed to see. I only needed a few more days.

I turned my attention to the next round of 'Wheel of Fortune,' reviewing the bids for the exclusive ownership of the Frau Graves' disfigurement footage—all cameras and still photos.

I sold off three more copies. Those funds would go into my Bogotá account after greasing their way through a few offshores, save 2.4 mil to make the film production nearly solvent.

I saw that Dice's Pet had replied to my third email requesting a forward look at the script for budgetary concerns.

It opened with, "Kindly go fuck yourself, per Dice."

I read no further. After a deep, calming breath, I wisely restrained myself from firing the hack. A brilliant idea came to me and wrote an email to studio security with a blind copy to my favorite scribe at the *National Inquisitor*.

"On the set of the new *Rascals* movie, it has been learned that screenwriter, Z. F. Glass, has a large cache of mutilation porn on her computer, including a collection of videos involving the terrible and graphic demise of young boys. It's believed that Dice, the film's director, is also involved. Please look into this."

Hitting send, I was pleased with myself. The scandal would lop off a head or two and distract the studio from their investigation of my books and other concerns.

With no more Z.F. Glass sucking on Dice's twanger and his dismissal a possibility, I left my desk. If they did call him back for *talks*, I knew the filming would continue. We could manage a few days without him, Touch likely filling in. They might even offer the chair to me. I had, after all, done an amazing job as director before a few unfortunate events. It wasn't likely but never expect lucid thinking from Hollywood.

I spent the next two hours in my bedroom with the library books and paper and pen interpreting the scientific and cautionary details into a practical and yes, beautiful sketch of the device.

Holes. Millions of holes. *A Holey Mess*. I decided I would use that title when I sold the A-List ending footage.

CHAPTER 19

Film Title: Rascals – The Donner *Party*
Production Day Twenty-Nine

*S*arah Graves woke mid-morning, groggy and frightened by the depth and length of her well-fed sleep. Wind was playing a childish melody in the pine needles and fabric of her makeshift tent. The sun gave off a look, if not feel, of warmth in the clear blue sky. Across the rocks and patches of soil was the fire pit, still filled with a rise of snow. Raising her head from her arm and pulling the bear pelt up over her tangled, dirty hair, she spoke into the current of wind.

"Fire pit. Fire. Go forward."

Having slept as she fell to her side, she rose on weak arms and sat up, scooting out from the tent into the cold morning wind. She gathered two arms full of twigs and branches and filled a coat pocket with pine cones. She shoveled out of the pit with her hands and laid in the wood. With the firebox found the day before, she tried to light a fire but couldn't get the damp twigs to ignite until she donated another land grant from inside her coat.

With the fire started, she spent half an hour caring for it, feeding the flames until it was strong enough to live on its own. She walked from the camp to scout out her next route. Her boots crunching on gray rock and gravel, she left the cover of the trees where the gusting winds pushed her side to side. A few minutes later, she stood before the western drop of the Sierras.

"There you are," she whispered, getting her first view of the promise of California.

Miles of mountains and valleys needed to be somehow navigated and traveled. At her boot toe was a vertical rock face falling three hundred feet with no possible cracks or rocks for foot and handholds.

"I don't see how." Her voice was disheartened but not discouraged. Others had somehow climbed to the windy perch. She returned to the tent for breakfast with renewed strength and improvement in spirit.

With a length of dried meat poking from her lips, she chewed until it was soft on her tongue and could be swallowed. After eating herself full, she fed the fire with two pine cones. Only then did she look across to the forward edge of the plateau. Climbing to her feet, she searched the ox crate and supply sacks for lengths of rope. She found a few, but even if she used those that elevated the sacks, there wasn't nearly enough.

The western drop would certainly kill her.

"Should I head south and then west?" She looked away from California.

"If only Stanton or whoever had left their ropes behind." She turned away, seeing something new at the back of the camp. Two crosses stood before six-foot lengths of piled rocks. The markers were made from boxwood and were nailed together. Her first thought was not of those who had died but greed for the wood.

She took a brief, furtive glance back in the direction she had come from the day before.

"Retreat?" she asked herself.

The question answered itself. She shook her head. Carrying the food sack back to those she had left behind would mean nothing more than a day or two of feeding their shrunken bellies. Then what? She also knew the answer to that.

Leaving the warmth of the fire, she walked to the southern edge of the plateau.

It offered an equally impossible drop of perhaps a thousand feet to a rocky basin.

"If I turn back, we'll all die." She lowered her head.

She began searching for possible handholds down the gray wall below, seeing a few dabs of grass poking out here and there. The winds were pushing at her, streaming her hair back from the scarred side of her face. She stepped closer to the edge for a better look for foot and handholds. Something touched her wrist and clenched. Startled, she jumped back and turned around.

Frau Graves' hand was locked on her coat sleeve.

"I wouldn't jump," the six-year-old said to her. "It might not kill you."

"I wasn't thinking of jumping." She stared at her sister pulling on her arm, leading her away. Sarah Graves dropped to her knees on the rocks and took Frau Graves in her arms.

"How? Why?" She hung on tight.

"You know the how," Frau Graves replied. "And the why is easy."

"All on your own?" Sarah Graves asked.

Instead of answering that, the child said, "I found this." She was holding out a folded piece of coarse stationery.

"Where?" Sarah Graves asked, unfolding the paper.

Frau Graves pointed to a stacked mound of rocks at the back of the southern drop. Sarah Graves had missed it completely. She read the coal chalked words.

> *We came for them but under supplied*
> *We will return better provisioned.*
> ~ *James Reed*

"HE'S the boy who was banished," Frau Graves said.

"And yet, he returned to help."

Sarah Graves recalled the banishment of James Reed for the murder of one-legged Snyder. The vote by the survivors and herself, only Frau Graves abstaining.

"We should've forgiven him." Frau Graves helped her sister to her feet. They started back to the camp, side by side, hand in hand.

"Yes, I wish I had." Sarah Graves lowered her eyes, struggling with regret.

"Come, let's get you inside the tent and feed you." She told her sister, seaking an escape from the recriminations icing her thoughts.

While Frau Graves ate dried meat and raw meal, she looked out from under the canvas canopy into the pines, planning each climb for dead and weak branches. With five possible limbs picked out, she eased from the tent to gather them.

Pulling a dead branch from a pine tree, a blanket of snow fell onto her face and shoulders. Shaking it off, she tugged again with all her strength, successfully breaking off the three-foot length of wet wood. Moving across the rocks to the next tree, she saw that she would have to climb. Movement to her left caught her eye. She stopped and stared. Another child was staggering into view. She recognized her, no matter the matted hair falling over her eyes. It was Wormy Girl from the last camp.

Margret Reed appeared next, looking much worse than before. She was shaking and stumbling, her eyes downcast and blinking rapidly in the final throws of starvation.

"Come. Eat." Sarah Graves led both girls to the tent where Frau Graves handed them strips of dried meat. The four girls sat in a circle under the canvas, the new arrivals eating as fast as they could, neither saying a word.

Ten minutes later, two more survivors climbed into view and crossed to the small camp. The first was Kesenberg followed by a smaller boy. Sarah Graves recognized him as one of the Donner Party members but didn't remember his name.

While they straggled to the fire and tent, Sarah Graves climbed out with food in her hands. She met the boys halfway and handed it to them. Neither had a word to say, too busy tearing the meat apart and chewing.

Margret Reed joined them, carrying a blanket she draped over the smaller boy, whose clothing was threadbare and soaked.

"Go to the tent," she told both.

Kesenberg dropped before the fire as the other boy crossed the rocks.

"I wasn't for this, but there was no hope left," Margret Reed said to Sarah Graves. "Some were too frail and sickly and had to be left behind."

"Things aren't much better here," Sarah Graves said.

"Whose camp is this?"

"Your brother's. He returned to help us all, but left, not having brought enough."

"My James…" Margret Reed stared at the scarred side of Sarah Graves' face, trying to catch her eye. "Trying to save us after all of you banished him."

"Yes, he's doing what he can to rescue us."

Turning away, Margret Reed spoke to the forward edge of the plateau.

"Tamzene Donner headed off down the mountain to rejoin her Uncle George at his Alder Lake camp. They'll surely perish. There's nothing to be had by retreating. Little more hope with this move forward."

"Come and eat some more. Thaw and warm yourself."

Turning to Kesenberg, she asked him to join them.

He shook his head, his hands at the edge of the flames.

Margret Reed followed in Sarah Graves' footsteps to the tent. Seated with the others, their backs blocked the worst of the freezing wind. Frau Graves handed out more pieces of dried meat. Sarah Graves declined the offer, having had breakfast.

Frau Graves tried to hand the nameless boy a fist full. His hand didn't open. Nudging him with her elbow, Sarah Graves turned to him.

"Eat, it'll restore you," she encouraged him.

The boy's head was draped by the blanket Margret Reed had given him. Sarah Graves leaned forward to see his face. His expression was blank and lost, his eyes to somewhere far away. She pressed the meat to the back of his hand. He didn't respond. She watched his lips for a wisp of breath. Not seeing one, she put her arm around him. His head dropped to his chest.

"No, no," she whispered, pulling him close.

His head lolled against her breast. The small nameless boy had escaped the icy hell they were trapped in.

Sarah Graves raised her eyes, tears welling. Frau Graves was watching her closely as she climbed to her feet.

Outside the tent, the fire was dwindling. Kesenberg was watching it, looking half dead. Minutes later, the flames began to crackle and spit as a piece of wood was laid in. There was a nail running through it and sap cooked off along its length. The second piece of the cross was in Frau Graves' hand, held at the ready.

Fade to black

CHAPTER 20

Truth or Consequences

I needed to stop in at Orosco's tool trailer to borrow a soldering iron for the lab, but first things first. With Glass the Pet being erased from my production, I headed over to Dice's editing den. I was dressed for my new role—black suit, white shirt, black tie, black socks, and wingtips. I was confident that word would come down soon and his name would be erased from the credits and possibly replaced with mine.

I knocked on Dice's door.

"Whoever it is, no!" was thrown back.

I entered, hoping to find Dice alone, unlikely as that was. He loved to work with a covey of like small minds.

Sure enough, Bear sat beside him with the film's composer on Dice's other side. I was surprised also to see Frau Graves, formerly SeaBee Danser. She and her mom

155

were on the couch behind the other three men. All were wide awake, no matter the hour—half-past one in the morning.

"Just got the news about the writer," I said to Dice. "Sorry for your loss."

"Shssh," the composer snarled at me. His name was Martuchi. Everyone called Martian. If Dice heard me, there was no indication. The three were shoulder to shoulder, speaking in clipped and coded conversation. Dice was pointing to the audio stream graphics and levels while Martian made fine adjustments.

I STARTED FEELING like a boy standing all alone in the shadows of a school dance. My hackles rose. Problem was, I hadn't brought along an ice breaker or hammer and chisel. There was nowhere to sit and I wasn't coming up with any way to include myself in their tight half-circle.

I took up a perch beside the couch, planning to dive in the first chance I got. I had a pitch to make, assuming they ever took a break.

A few minutes later, I moved closer, standing at their backs. I leaned over, pretending interest in the playbacks and edits. Martian was explaining to Dice how the new music was going to add a darker texture to the visuals.

"Adding emotional temperature, but the levels are too high." He slid one of the soundboard levers.

"There, play that back," he told Bear. "Last thing we want is the audience sensing the manipulation and fall out of the story."

Dice listened closely, rubbing his chin, considering, not committing. Bear leaned forward, eyes roving up and down along the three streams of footage for the twelve and a half seconds they were editing, evaluating each for angle and frame size. The air around their heads smelled like a fruit bowl—all three were vaping. Dice was actually touching the mouse and keyboard, something I had never done as a director, leaving that to those beneath my grade.

"I agree. Great. Thank you," Dice told Martian after the new music levels played under the footage.

"Got the memo about Glass," he said to me, not turning. "Makes me sad. In this industry, she's dropped for looking at a few pictures. I'm sure they were for some film research. Well, somewhat sure."

"Yes, it's an unfortunate and important loss," I said. "I'm sure you must feel—"

"If your hand was in it, I'll have you castrated."

"Trust me, I had no idea. Security must have—"

"Flor? Why are you here? What do you want?"

"I want to suggest a replacement. My *Lost Cabin in the Forest* writer."

"That hack with one decent chop?"

I needed to have the *hack* hired and flown in fast. If I got him on board, I'd have access to the script.

"So, pitch," Dice sounded irritated and hostile, displeased by the distraction from the editing.

"This story needs his detached, unemotional style. He can improve the film and make it artistically relevant."

"Sounds like Flor wants to do another version of his *Cabin* failure." Bear leaned back, expelling a cloud of vape smoke my way.

"IMDB said you have 'the vision of a sheet cake.' *Lost Cabin in the Forest* is void of violence, blood, or drama. A shallow attempt at art that fails because of a lack of passion and vision. One hour and ten minutes of bland and soggy milk toast."

I was impressed that he had read and memorized that. The insult bounced off my armor, and I remained focused.

"He has the gift. *Cabin* wasn't all his fault." I stop way short of admitting who was to blame.

"Fly him in, I'll talk with him. You won't be in the room." Dice ended the conversation, rejoining Bear and Martian at work on the edit of those twelve and a half seconds.

Martian stood and called for a break a few minutes later.

"I need to run through the ADR steps with Frau Graves, so she's ready," he said, turning and smiling to the child on the couch.

ADR stands for Automated Dialog Replacement. It's often used when dialog can't be salvaged from the production tracks, or as in this case, to overdub the former star's voice with the new star, SeaBee Danser.

"We go with the medium-framed shot. The most inclusive," Dice decided, still focused on the monitors.

Bear marked the selected clip and stored it. Dice turned his chair around to Frau Graves, putting on his kind and caring mask. Martian sat beside the child and her mom, all smiles and fawning.

"Martian here is going to explain the re-recording process," Dice spoke to the child. "We want your lovely voice to replace the other in the earlier scenes."

Turning to me, all sweetness was gone.

"I want a press kit put together for this darling. I want her signed by dawn."

To Sara, the mom, he cooed, "You're good?"

"After I talk it out with Pauline, yes." The tan and good-looking young woman nodded.

A stick in the spokes, but I had taken care of it. Pauline Place had been smoothed. All she wanted for her granddaughter was a hideous amount of money and an ungodly three points of proceeds. The press kit was completed back in Los Angles. I had insisted it play up the kid's 'lineage of stardom.'

"Have a question." The newly-formed star put on her top hat and veil. "Will I get to taste the dead people?"

Dice shook his head, delighted and amused.

My cell phone purred. I took it out and saw a text from the detective.

There's security footage of you entering the armory the night before Trenton's accident. You've got some serious explaining to do. Can't wait to hear it. You WILL be in my office tomorrow morning.

A LINK to a video was attached. I hit play and a black and white clip started. It showed me empty-handed but walking with a stiff-legged limp. As it should, the replacement musket was shoved down my pant leg.

I could avoid him no longer. It was time to take his meaty fat hand and lead him through the explanation—my insomnia and arthritic knees.

"Why are you standing there?" Dice said to me. "You've got work to do."

I left the RV, phone in hand. A voicemail had also come in. Walking to my RV, I tapped play.

It was from fat, biscuit-stuffed Roy. I hit play.

"We figure you're trying to milk the insurance or studio or doing some fancy math for a big payday. We want our cut."

I didn't reply. I needed the rest of the night to finish my machine. I would swing by his wrecking yard after I dealt with the detective, then Roy and I could play a round of *Truth or Consequences.*

CHAPTER 21

Film Title: Rascals – The Donner *Party*
Production Day: Thirty

*S*arah and Frau Graves walked away from the others around the fire and inside the sad excuse of a tent, working downhill through the pines, gathering what little wood they could find. In her top hat and veil, Frau Graves proved herself more than capable of climbing for dead branches and limbs, no matter her obscured vision. Reaching the northern end of the strand of trees, Sarah Graves stepped back as her sister dropped a dead, five-foot branch. It crashed to the rocks as Frau Graves climbed higher.

"We'll work the west side next," Sarah Graves called up to her.

Frau Graves climbed like a squirrel out on a limb and dropped to the one below. She jumped and fell six feet through the air, landing on her feet at her sister's side.

Listening to the whisper of the pine needles on the rocks

as Frau Graves dragged the tree branch to the fire, Sarah Graves walked in the opposite direction. She wanted to take a second to look down the cliff face that James Reed had climbed. Standing at the edge and looking down, she saw what had escaped her before. Off to the left was a twenty-foot drop to a ledge. Below it was a second outcropping.

"We might have enough rope for those," she spoke to the possible new route, walking over to it.

Under the outcropping was a dangerous decline, but not straight up and down. A path suggested itself running down through boulders and frozen brush. Further below was a ravine wandering to the west.

"You braved this for us," she thanked James Reed.

Another thought came to mind, the cause of their current near-death situation.

"Hastings, you foul quim," she accused through clenched teeth.

"I see another kid," Frau Graves called out from behind, her voice torn by the wind.

Sarah Graves turned to see who the new arrival was. The flat rock under her feet cracked and gave away. Throwing her arms out, she teetered, her hands grasping nothing but thin air. Bits of shale clacked and tumbled.

"No!" she screamed. Losing her balance, she fell.

Minutes later, Kesenberg and Francis Donner tied a length of camp rope to a tree trunk and dropped it to where Sarah Graves lay unmoving on the ledge. Frau Graves insisted on being the first to descend, boots kicking the rock face, little hands clenched to the rope. Kesenberg followed her down with a second length of rope coiled over his shoulder.

Frau Graves kneeled beside her sister and swept her bloody hair back from the three-inch-long gash on the scarred side of her face. Blood was pulsing from the wound.

Her sister was unconscious, eyes blank and opened wide. Ignoring her sibling's black, swollen eye, Frau Graves pressed her coat sleeve to the deep cut on the landscape of scar tissue, trying to stem the flow.

Kesenberg dropped to her side and handed her a scrap of table linen. Frau Graves pressed it to the injury. Watching the cloth redden, she used the loose ends to wrap and secure the cloth around her sister's head.

"Her foot." Kesenberg pointed to Sarah Graves' ankle, which was twisted at a sickly angle.

"That's next," Frau Graves replied. Cold winds were shoving at them. The dangerous side of the ledge was only a couple of feet away.

Placing her ear to Sarah Graves' lips, she listened for a breath. Her head low and turned to the side, she watched Kesenberg gently work the second rope under Sarah Graves' back. A faint breath of warm air came from her sister's lips.

Lifting her as little as possible, Kesenberg slid the rope under Sarah Graves.

Frau Graves kept her face close to her sister's, silently willing her to hold on. Kesenberg tied and knotted the drop line to the rope around Sarah Graves' upper body.

Testing the knot with a hefty pull on the drop line, he raised the rope slowly. Seeing Sarah Graves' upper body rise a few inches, he lowered her back onto the rocks and started his climb back up the granite cliff face.

"Stay with me," Frau Graves whispered to her sister before turning away. She followed Kesenberg up the face of the cliff, the coarse rope burning and blistering her palms and small fingers.

Working together, Frau Graves, Kesenberg, and Francis Donner worked the line, slowly dragging their stricken and still silent leader up the twenty-foot drop. The three carried her to the camp and lay her inside the tent, Frau Graves donating her pelt for comfort and warmth. With the other children watching on, scared and silent, she carefully raised her sister's head and rested it in her lap.

"We can't lose her," Wormy Girl broke the silence, letting out a sob.

The others whispered among themselves, a few also crying.

Frau Graves turned her veiled eyes to them, her jaw set, her voice firm.

"Bring me some snow. I'm going to get my sister to drink."

Kesenberg climbed out to do so. The other children looked helpless and stricken, staring on through their tears. Frau Graves turned her attention back to her sister, looking into her blank eyes and expression.

Kesenberg returned with a handful of snow and handed it across. Frau Graves held it in the cup of her hands, breathing in and out fast. The first drop to fall landed between Sarah Graves' lips. Seconds later, another fell. Panting warm air again and again, Frau Graves never paused until only her red palms showed.

"Break me off a small bit of meat," she ordered, not looking up from her sister.

Margret Reed handed her a sliver of dried beef and Frau Graves put it in own her mouth. Chewing until it was soft, she slid the small red gob in between her sister's lips.

"What are we to do?" Wormy Girl let out a cry, hands clenched together at her chest.

"We're going to stop asking questions like that." Frau Graves aimed her veiled eyes at her.

Turning to Kesenberg, she told him, "Go see to the fire. The rest of you get some sleep. It's going to be a long, cold night."

Dawn brought ugly gray clouds that boiled and released

an ice-filled rain. The fire was extinguished in the down-pour, those around it running for cover. Those who couldn't find space in the tent cowered under the trees.

An hour later, the fire pit was filled with slush and water. Calling everyone together, Margret Reed handed out the last of the food supplies. Listless, forlorn eyes watched her hands, the faces slack and thin from hunger.

Frau Graves and Francis Donner remained at Sarah Graves' side inside the tent, keeping a silent vigil. She had neither stirred or spoken through the night.

As rain and ice formed channels across the rocky camp, the last two members of the Donner group, boys of eight and nine, got to their feet after stirring through the supply sack. Without a word or glance for approval from the others, they crossed to the body of the last boy to die, carrying a knife and saw.

That evening, everyone ate. With renewed strength, a second, larger tent of sorts was built with lengths of table linen and rope. This shelter was set up in the east edge of the camp where the cover of the trees was the densest. The children climbed inside, the opening facing the other tent where Sarah Graves, Frau Graves, and Francis Donner lay bunched close to one another.

Frau Graves replaced Sarah Graves' bandage with a new one, dabbing at the wound first, the bleeding had stopped, but the gash was raw and ugly. Francis Donner watched on, eyes dull and unfocused until Frau Graves completed the change.

"At least she kept the meat down," Frau Graves said to her, the veil softening her voice.

Francis Donner nodded as Frau Graves lay down beside her sister. Francis Donner's lips and chin, like Frau Graves', were dappled with blood from the dead boy.

Midway through the third day since her fall, Sarah Graves raised her head and strained to rise onto her elbows. With slight strength and lucidity returned, she saw that her sister and Francis Donner were sleeping at her sides. Finding a bit more energy to sit up all the way, she looked out from the tent through the sheets of hard, falling rain. She saw the other tent for the first time, the faces inside looking haunted and lost. On the rocks between the two shelters were trails of blood. Even with the rains trying to wash the stones, the stains remained.

Looking at the faces across the way, she used her fingers to gently explore the deep cut on her cheekbone and the swelling around that same eye. Sliding her tongue through her cut and flaked lips, she tasted a salty residue. Her fingertips brushed her lips and chin and came away with blood that was still warm.

Filled with revulsion, her stomach clenched.

"No, no." She had held out for so long.

Outside, the rain stopped, replaced by falling, spiraling snow.

Leaning out, she saw where the dead boy had been dragged to. A cross rose from a mound of rocks at the back of his head, his calves and thighs sliced to the bone.

"It's come to this." It wasn't a question but the start of acceptance.

The fire in the circle of rocks was burning, smoke gathering under the draped canvas. Kesenberg sat before it, alone, a stick in his hand. He was stirring the inside of a bowl made of bear pelt hanging from a branch. She could smell the boiling gruel.

Turning away, she saw a second body, one of the two Donner Party boys. He lay a few yards off to the right, snowflakes coming to rest on his open eyes and mouth. His body was fully clothed, so far not fed on.

"You're back among us." Her sister touched her arm, her voice innocent and strangely playful.

Sarah Graves tried to see her eyes through the black veil, looking for a sign of her health and sanity. There was nothing to be seen.

"Are you okay, my darling?" she asked.

Her sister was looking out through the opening where the snow was coming down hard.

Frau Graves' next words were light and conversational.

"When I get to California, I'm going to fill a basket with peaches and morning flowers."

Fade to black

CHAPTER 22

The Roar

I finished the revised contract for SeaBee Danser at four in the morning and fired it off to the studio for their sprinkling of holy water. After a nap on the bed beside Darryl, I showered and used the borrowed soldering iron to complete the last connections on my invention. When all the wires were connected, I wrapped the device in black silk from the fabric store. Pocketing my shopping list, I went and checked out a loaner Land Rover.

Entering the bank right at nine o'clock, I cut a studio check for a second twenty-thousand dollars, this time without the minimum-wage hag trying to slow me up. I was better prepared for the ghastly lights of Walmart, wearing a pair of wrap-around shades. Holding my list and checking it twice, I steered my shopping cart into Electronics for a burner cell phone. Next was the Men's section for crappy and cheap clothing, including a pair of clod-kicking low boots. I rolled through Toys, Hardware, and Sporting Goods filling my cart. Next up was Women's Clothing for a handbag, where I was delighted to find one with fake black silk lining, unnecessary, but a nice touch. After paying with cash, I rolled away from those mole-eyed shoppers and life-stunned clerks.

Inside the Rover, I changed into the dull-colored clothing for my hick-farmer look. I expected my new look to put Roy and his boys at ease. While the GPS on the dash figured out the route to his large barn and farmhouse, I entered his number from my cell phone into the burner. With his number saved, I reviewed my plan one last time. It was time to deal with their dull-headed attempt at blackmail. Dealing with the detective had to wait.

Out in the country, I drove the two-lane roads through miles of green fields and grain silos. Here and there were farmhouses looking like they had tipped over the edge into poverty. The gray clouds overhead gave everything a look of lifelong futility. Wake, hoe weeds, die. I shook my head at their stupidity.

Pulling into the long driveway through Roy's wrecking yard, I hit the dial on the burner.

"Yeah," Roy answered.

"I want to buy another brick and discuss the other business."

"I see your car. Come on up."

I parked fifteen yards back from the barn, packed the Walmart purse, and climbed out into the freezing wind. Crossing the frozen mud and gravel, there was Roy, standing just inside the barn. One of his fellow fat friends stood beside him. Roy Two was dressed for wit, his open denim jacket displaying a stained 'GOT FUCK?' t-shirt. Roy One was in dirty serge coveralls. Both look haggard, like they just woke up if they ever did so.

"Nice purse, gay boy," Roy Two said.

I let that go.

I didn't see the third man from before, Roy Three, the scrawny meth sucker. This was unfortunate but workable. He was surely close by with a farm animal, trousers dropped.

"I brought you six thousand for another brick and ten thousand for your silence," I handed over the purse.

"Feels good and heavy," Roy took it and looked inside. "Ten is a good start."

"Thought so."

"Go get him a second," he told Roy Two.

While he disappeared in the shadows of the barn, I considered Roy's dumb unshaven face.

"A good start? Figured as much," I said.

"We're easy to work with. You're now on our installment plan."

He was doing his best to look like a tough guy, there in his mud-splattered coveralls and grease-stained hands.

"Do you have a bottom-line number?" I asked.

"We'll get back to you on that."

Roy Two came out with another brick in a reused plastic shopping bag. I took it and walked back to the Rover. There is nothing left to be said or discussed. Sitting behind the wheel, I watched those two opening the purse and staring inside. Pleased, I imagined.

I drove all the way through the wrecking yard and out to their gate before I pushed the remote-control button.

The roar was magnificent. The Rover rocked forward and back on its springs. All I could see in the rearview mirror was rising, twisting black smoke over scattered fires. Putting the car in reverse, I backed up between the stacks of smashed automobiles. When I was thirty yards from the barn, I braked and turned around on the seat.

As planned, my invention has worked perfectly. Smoke

was boiling and climbing from the fires. The front half of the barn was blown in, fire consuming the rest. Before it was a deep hole in the dirt and gravel where they had last stood. Off to the right was one of their trucks. Looking along its length, I was more than pleased. Its windows were blown out and the tires were flattened. The ruined fender, door, and bed side all repulsed and demanded I look closer. It wasn't the splash of blood and bits from their bodies, but the pattern of thousands of deep tiny holes pockmarking the metal.

CHAPTER 23

Film Title: Rascals – The Donner *Party*
Production Day: Thirty-One

*W*hen Frau Graves returned empty-handed from her search for firewood, those who could stand from around the circle of rocks did so and climbed into the second tent. The reality of the loss of fire shown in their faces and all talk of escape ended as though their fate was secured. The weak, starving children sat in their tight quarters, packed close together.

Inside the first smaller tent, Frau Grave and Francis Donner hemmed Sarah Graves, who sat with her chin on her knees staring across the rocks at the opening of the other tent. Dried blood was flaked on the ruined side of her face. Francis Donner's head was down. She was in restless sleep, her lips red from fresh blood twitching within a shallow dream. Frau Graves was staring straight up at the tent top, her eyes veiled.

GREG JOLLEY

Seeing the last Donner boy climb out with a knife and saw, Sarah Graves closed her eyes.

Ground-pounding thunder boomed from close overhead and the camp was struck brilliant white with a crack of lightning. Minutes later, the clouds opened, and rain fell, heavy with ice.

Within the next half hour, the plateau they were perched on was running with freezing streams and rivers through the shale and stones.

THE DONNER BOY crawled inside the girls' tent. His clothing was drenched, and he held slices of uncooked flesh with stringy veins and gristle.

"No thank you," Sarah Graves told him. Her hunger was strong and yelling at her, but she would hold out until it screamed. Frau Graves accepted the meat and nodded once in gratitude. The boy kneeled backward out into the torrent and returned to what little remained of his unburied friend.

Frau Graves placed the meat in the fold of her lap and tore a coin-size piece off.

"We need your strength," she whispered to her sister, placing the meat before her mouth. Closing her eyes, Sarah Graves parted her lips and accepted.

The rains let up and snow started falling with the onset of darkness. Frau Graves gently pressed her sister onto her back and lay down close beside her. Francis Donner did the same on the other side, the three facing the night in a tight embrace for what little warmth they could share.

The sky was white with low clouds when Frau Graves stirred the next morning. The view through the opening in the canvas was a frozen relief—all rocks and trees and the second tent glazed with thick ice on top of snow. In the pine trees, daggers of icicles hung from the limbs. She pressed a remaining ball of gristle into her coat pocket and scooted forward, the two other girls not stirring.

Extending her head out into the freezing winds, she raised her veil-covered eyes to the sky, baring her teeth, her lips and chin covered with dried blood. Addressing the sky and heaven above, she snarled wordlessly and climbed out.

In the still and silent clearing between the two shelters, she picked a pair of snowshoes and the coil of rope used to retrieve her sister after her fall. With the rope in her hand, she left the camp, stumbling on weak legs across the snow and ice. Minutes later, she stood before the twenty-foot drop to what her sister said was the James Reed trail ahead.

"My turn to try." She tied off the rope to a tree trunk and tossed the length over.

Fade to black

CHAPTER 24

Black Silk

*D*arryl and his girlfriend were nesting as far as possible from the laboratory, finding cover on the floor mat of the passenger seat in the front of the RV. Hard to blame him or her, the fumes from one squeeze after another of superglue were an offensive, eye-stinging stench.

Emptying four tubes of that noxious glue, I placed the brick in the platter of BBs and turned it over and over. Opening more tubes of glue and pouring out another mound of the tiny steel balls, I repeated the process, adding a second layer. Four rounds later, the brick was fat with thousands of tiny projectiles. By then, my eyes were watering, and my mind was elevated over my body, hovering. There were people who sniffed that stuff for fun, having themselves a 'party.' The effect on me was far from festive. I heard a curtain hem slide across stage planks and received a vision that stopped my work.

I was visiting a morgue for identification purposes. Before me was a steel autopsy table. I was alone, pulling back a black silk sheet draped over an amazing, seductive female body. The woman's head was turned away, her expensively coiffed hair matted with blood. Her body was covered with hundreds of tiny round entrance wounds. With her magnificently beautiful face turned to the side, she still welcomed me. Pauline Place lay on her belly, ass up, offering herself.

My hand swept the bedding, batting the tubes of glue onto the floor. Kneeling and holding my breath, I picked them up and dumped them inside a plastic bag and knotted it tight. I left the RV for a few minutes of fresh air before returning to work.

The second device looked a little different from the one I had used on Roy and friends. An antenna rose from the brick and detonator attached to the C-clamp I would secure it with. All that was left to do was wire in the signal receiver. When I was halfway done with that, I decided I had to air out the RV as the glue fumes still lingered. Opening the door, frigid air braced me. Darryl dashed out sans his little woman and started spinning in circles, yapping. The dog was clearly high or deranged.

After letting him spin himself senseless, I got him back inside and finished my invention. I wrapped the device in black silk and headed over to the third set—the one for the zoom shot from the tower.

We were scheduled for a nine o'clock shoot, which meant that the film crews had been at work for hours. While the pampered cast slumbered in their fine beds, the technicians prepped and placed cameras as the audio and lighting crews worked through their setups and tests. Weaving the equipment and snaking cables, I searched for my new screenwriter, whose balls and career were in the grip of my hands.

He looked nervous and frightened as I approached,

always a good sign. He was holding that day's script on a clipboard, which I reached for.

He actually resisted.

"I can't release a copy to you," he chattered, eyes scanning fast, left to right.

"Then answer this. They're prepping the third set for the camera drop. Is this an A-list group shot?"

"Yes, we're going out of sequence. The weather forecast is showing strong winds coming in tomorrow."

I gave the forty-something writer my dagger eyes, reminding him that his once-in-a-lifetime career chance could be extinguished at my whim.

"What do you have there?" he braved, eyes to the black-draped device, the size of a loaf of rye.

I walked away without another word, his question and existence tiresome. On the edge of the set, I upended one of the electrician's grip bags, dumping tools and parts out and sliding the device inside and shouldering it. Before entering the hallowed ground of the set, I needed to plant my alibi with Orosco. He was standing at the base of the camera tower.

"I'm going up to see the new Panavision the DP *had* to purchase and ship for this. Another obscene expense."

"Climb carefully and cable yourself off up top," he advised.

"Will do." I crossed to the steel ladder rising to the camera and lighting crew high up on the catwalk.

One of my many talents was having no fear of heights. I climbed steadily, looking down at the distance between my body and the solid-set flooring. Up top, I cabled to my belt loop and walked out to where the new Panavision and a grip and cameraman were running tests beside the open lens and power cases. These two were dialed into their work and didn't look up as I eased past to the center of the catwalk for a revealing and magical view of the set below.

The foot-long Xs on the stage floor were in three different colors of gaffer tape, identifying the positions of the A-listers for the start of the shot. The scene was on the riverbank below. Three sides of the set were armed with AARI lights and reflection panels and diffusers, none of the lights yet struck. At the edge of the stage, the chairs for the primes were set out for Dice, Touch, and Bear. They were placed so those three had a clear view of the action in between Cameras Two and Three. Boom mics crisscrossed the air over the set and between the audio soundboard and chairs, the multi-camera monitor workstations were glowing, ready to receive footage from the three cameras. Once the wind machines were fired up, the shot would be ready and the cast would get their call.

All in all, it was a masterful complex of equipment and crews at the ready, prepared to spend four to five hours capturing less than a minute of action and dialogue. The tension would soon ramp up with a silent electrical buzz when Dice and entourage appeared. There would be instructions and clipped Q & A with the crew leads before the cast took their places.

From a hundred feet up, it was a satisfying visage, like gazing down from heaven, where soon hell would be delivered by thousands of tiny steel BBs. Studying the Panavision mounting on the camera track, I saw where I could attach the C-clamp to its lower motor housing.

"Flor? What are you doing up here?" the cameraman asked, kneeling at the open lens case.

"Need to see what eighty thousand bought." I pretended to be giving the camera a closer look. I needed him and the grip to stop monkeying with the camera and move to the tower controls at the far side of the catwalk.

"It bought the best. The DP considered using two Kinetta's but needed the lower aspect and DOF..."

I tuned him out, nodding along at the rest of his babble like I admired and comprehended the tech gibberish.

"Test," the grip said, and the two left the camera for the control board and monitor fifteen feet across the walk. I waited until they were halfway across before taking the device from the tool bag and securing the clamp to the camera mount inside the tangle of cables. It was hidden well, as I had planned.

Standing up, I leaned over the railing for another glance below into the busy and complicated equipment and crews at work around the set and the three blue, green, and red Xs. A flush of delight filled and elevated my brain like a balloon. I had a vision that made my palms sweat on the aluminum railing. A roaring explosion and flash of blinding light. The crews and the primes would freeze in disbelief a second later. Before them, in the center of the three-sided circle, the A-listers stood for a third of a second before the thousands of tiny holes in their faces and bodies begin to pulse and fill with their own blood.

After climbing down from the tower, I left to get Darryl. I wanted him in my arms when I pushed the remote-control button.

CHAPTER 25

Film Title: Rascals – The Donner *Party*
Production Day: Thirty-Two

Frau Graves let go of the rope and stepped around the blood-stained rocks from her sister's fall, the splatters discolored by layers of ice. Below the ledge was the second drop of twenty feet. The pitch was steep and she had no choice except to start down facing the cold granite, struggling for footholds. Her red, stinging hand locked onto anything she could grasp as she made her way a third of the way down. At that point, her boot toes could find nothing to balance on below or to the side. With no other choice, she let go. Sliding down, her chest, knees, and ribs were scraped and bashed before her boots struck the rocks below.

Having tumbled backward onto her rear on impact, she saw and ignored her cut and bleeding legs. Out before her to the right was the only possible route. As she headed out, her small fists clenched in her pockets, one burrowing for warmth and the other around the ball of greasy human flesh. Leaning forward against the wind, looking out through her veil, she stepped out on the foot-wide ledge leading to rocks and trees in the distance. She inched along, the shear, deadly drop at her heels.

When she reached the end, she had no choice but to jump down. Landing hard, she sank to her hips in the snow under its crust of ice. Dunking low, she started tunneling forward, surrounded by the freezing white walls she was forming with her hands. Half an hour later, her left hand struck a rock. She dug at its sides, finding no way around. Stepping back, she cleared its uneven face, and without a pause, climbed. Bashing her head upward, she cracked the ice and pulled herself up onto its top.

The other side of the snow-covered rock ran like a ridgetop to a strand of trees. Carefully taking one step at a time, she pressed her heel down through the ice and snow until it pressed against stone. Reaching the end, she jumped off, sinking a few feet in. Hunkered low, she took the snow-shoes off her back and put them on. Half an hour later, she was under a tree and standing on frozen dirt.

There were no signs of life, no footprints, no broken twigs, or marked rocks to suggest the way. She pressed on through the trees, one step after another for an hour. Coming to a clearing surrounded by boulders, she removed the snowshoes. Crossing over to the end of the level ground, there was no way forward except another steep descent. She butt-scooted down the iced rock face, slowing herself when-ever she could with her heels and hands. At the bottom, she stood before a snow-covered meadow.

Putting the snowshoes back on, she started across. The thick inches of ice on top of the snow made the crossing a slow and exhausting struggle. Entering a shroud of dense pines with the winds held at bay, Frau Graves came to a stop.

Fighting off the urge to eat, she pushed a few handfuls of snow into her mouth, letting it melt in her warm mouth before filling her belly with unsatisfying cold water.

She wove her way downhill through the trees, making a good mile before noon. Standing in frozen mud under a hundred-foot pine, before her was a steep hill bordered by steep drops on both sides. The harsh winds were shoving her, trying to knock her down. She looked again for any sign of life and saw none. Beyond the hill was nothing but endless miles of lower mountains running to the west. The view would be beautiful if not so deadly and threatening.

Pushing off the tree, her chattering teeth were clenching and clicking. Taking one step and then another, she descended the hill. Refusing to let her head droop as it wanted to, she kept her veiled eyes forward for whatever challenge she had to face next.

Hours later, she came upon a strand of trees and entered. Removing the snowshoes, she trudged the mud and rocks until she was a hundred yards in. With nightfall approaching, she ate half of the meat in her pocket, her back pressed to the rough bark of an oak tree. Sliding down onto her haunches, she gave in to the desperate urge for sleep and closed her eyes.

She woke as she had slept, back against the oak, knees raised. Before her and to her sides, the trees reached out forever. A dense fog blocked the sun, taking away her sense of direction. Looking back along her snowshoe marks in the mud and kicked rocks, she chose her forward path by rounding the oak tree and trying for a continuing straight line.

A hundred yards out, she came to a stop, staring at the mud and gravel. After quickly looking side to side, she kneeled and raised her veil. There was a muddy footprint.

She saw the next and a third and lowering her veil, she

followed. Wanting to hurry, but too weak to do so, she followed one print to the next, the slightest of smiles showing under the hem of the veil.

Coming to a downward clearing, the footprints were joined by oxen hoof marks and wheel ruts to their sides. Looking up for the first time since spotting the first boot mark, she saw two felled trees, the stumps cut chest high. Against one was an abandoned supply box. She picked it up and carried it forward.

"Firewood," she spoke, her tiny voice husky.

The camp was abandoned but supplied. An open wagon was off to the left, the oxen bridles fallen to the ground. Boxes and furniture were stacked in the back of the wagon. Frau Graves spun and scanned the trees above, spotting two elevated food stashes.

Unknotting the line to the first, she lowered the sack to the ground and took five mouthfuls of raw flour, coughing and chewing and swallowing. Closing the flour bag, she pulled out a second and ate dried strips of beef. Using the box she had carried from the clearing, she sat on it and ate, pausing only to scoop up snow to drink. She ate until her belly ached and began cramping. Waiting for the pain to pass, she studied the camp.

The cook fire was filled with leaves and soggy gray embers. A few feet back from it, a man-made stack of shale formed a tower. At the head was a round stone holding down an empty seed bag. Removing the stone and opening it, she unfolded the note inside.

THIS FORWARD CAMP *needs resupply before the final ascent.*
   Will return in a fortnight.
   James Reed

. . .

POCKETING THE NOTE, Frau Graves retraced her footsteps through the trees until she stood between the two sawed tree trunks. Looking up, there stood the mountain she had come down. She traced what she could see of her prior path.

"A three-day climb," she whispered, her tongue swollen by the tang of the dried beef.

Returning to the dropped food sack, she lifted it with a grunt and struggled it onto her shoulder.

"The light." She frowned, looking at the long shadows before her.

Rather than start the climb in the approaching darkness, she released the sack to the ground.

"Start up at dawn." She turned away.

Climbing onto the wagon, she opened two long boxes of supplies before finding what she needed. Leaving the wagon, she filled her pockets with dried meat before hoisting the food sack back into the tree. With the evening light draining fast, she climbed back onto the wagon and squeezed in between the boxes, draping herself with the coarse horse blanket.

Lowering her head to the plank boards, she heard the distant creak of wood straining against metal. Sitting up fast, she stared into trees, seeing no movement, no sign of whatever had caused the sound. Then from deep in the trees, a child's voice groused, a single word followed by more moans of wood and steel.

"Gettalong."

Fade to black

CHAPTER 26

Stricken

"*L*eash that," Dice growled at Darryl, who was sniffing and growling at his shoes.

I scooped up my little companion, wanting to bite Dice's head and testicles off, but wisely restrained myself. We were standing before the third set, the river bank with waist-high grass swaying in the winds from three of Orosco's large blowers.

My eyes tracked upward along the camera tower to the Panavision and my device.

"Striking lights," Touch yelled, and the set was transformed by the lamps and diffusion panels to the hues of a warm, golden California sunset. The cast was on their marks, poised for their lines and moves, their gaunt and pale young faces looking almost hopeful. The lighting composition included orange and yellow flickers off the river.

Dice walked the stars through the shot three times, asking

for adjustments to pace and gestures. The children gave Dice their full attention. Sarah Graves, James Reed, and the veiled Frau Graves listened carefully as he directed them in a kind voice, modifying their inflections and expressions.

Off the set a few feet back, beautiful and elusive Pauline Place watched her granddaughter through the swaying grass. I looked away from her to the camera tower and couldn't help but smile. My estimate of the blast pattern included her as well as the primes and much of the surrounding crew.

Dice called for a fourth walk-through, this time asking that the zoom camera be dropped. He bumped past me to stand in front of the large monitor where the live footage displayed from all three cameras. I followed also to look. As the Panavision lowered, the cast on the riverbank went through their lines and movements. The tower camera stopped ten feet over their heads, where the operator manually completed the zoom.

I saw how all three cameras would capture the blast and aftereffects.

"Again!" Dice commanded, frowning at the monitors.

The Panavision was raised and Touch and Dice closed ranks, discussing timing, composition, and lighting. On the set, the cast relaxed, forced to make small talk with each other. Bear joined the two men, hand on Dice's shoulder as the three started another round of their private buddy yakking. I stepped back, unwelcomed and unnoticed.

Looking away from the set, I chose the equipment crate I'd crouch behind for protection. The one I selected was behind where Pauline Place and Frau Graves' mother stood watching the child star. I walked over to a production assistant and handed Darryl to him, saying, "Put him in my Mercedes."

"Not my job, bro."

"It is now, fuckface."

He shook his head and walked away.

Pauline Place overheard and glared at me, displeased with my breaking the spell. I was smitten by the direct eye contact, no matter the hostility. Her hair had been dyed an Irish red for her role, adding to her beauty.

"Quiet on the set," Touch yelled.

The soft verbal buzz among the crews stopped immediately.

"Let's get this," Dice called.

"Striking," the lights lead called.

"Audio *rolling*."

"Speeding," Bear yelled after confirming all three cameras were running.

The slater stepped in front of Camera Two and clacked the electronic clapper, calling out, "Donner Party, shot one-forty-six, take one."

As always, Dice called out, "Ready" and paused for a few seconds, studying his creation. "Action!" he shouted.

The actors and actresses began the scene. I was struck by how much they were like puppets on strings being guided through a farce. The tower camera glided downward as the cast spoke their initial lines while moving to their marks from different directions—Sarah and Frau Graves center, Francis Donner joining them from behind alongside a girl with a long rifle. Her presence in the scene was a surprise, and I cursed the secretly held script.

As the A-listers stood together with the artificial lights off the river dabbing their faces, Dice stood up from beside Camera Two and called out, "Cut!"

He entered the scene, stepping into the lights and wind from the fans.

"Good," he said to the cast. "We go again."

Eye to eye with Sarah Graves, his gaze intense, he let a smile play out, saying, "Next time, when you reach inside your coat to reassure yourself you've got the deeds, I want your eyes across the river, not on your hand. Your singular focus is Hastings across the water."

Back in place next to Camera Two and its secondary viewfinder display, Dice bobbed his head one time in Touch's direction, not looking up.

"Places," Touch yelled.

Audio, lights, and camera crews called out, confirming they were running. The slate was cracked and read out.

"Ready…" Dice called. "Action!"

The second take was a choreographed dance of crew and cast. The tower camera was halfway down, and the take was forty seconds in when Dice stood again.

"Cut! That was better. We go again."

He had an issue with the breeze in the grass—it was too strong, and he wanted it waving. As one of Orosco's crew members adjusted the fans, Dice knelt before Frau Graves and politely and kindly explained how he wanted her hand on the knife to tighten and squeeze on the hilt.

The third shot ran to the first word of dialog from Sarah Graves when "Cut" was called. Dice wants a different inflection. "Make the anger boil over. Squinting mad. Your eyes hot on Hastings. Give me your tight teeth."

She processed the changes and ran through them twice, experimenting with nuance. Dice squeezed her arm, saying, "You're nailing it. Great work," and returned to his place.

"Again," he called, and Touch took over, calling for and receiving the ready call out from the crews. The revised slate was struck, and the scene started over.

The fourth take was interrupted before Fancis Donner and the hunter girl reached Sarah and Frau Graves. Dice wanted the light diffuser on the right side 750 lamp closed to sharpen its light. He and Bear discussed the change, Bear deferring but sharing his concern with face shine and shadows. Dice listened intensely, hand on chin. A moment later, he agreed, and the lamp was returned to its original opened side panels.

"Fine work, all. One more time," Dice called, and while no one braved a word, there were a few terse grins. The promise of *one more time*, implying the last would certainly be broken.

Take five ran through to completion.

"*Cut*. Great stuff, all. Brilliant. That was perfect. We go again."

While crew and cast prepared for the sixth take, I carried Darryl over beside the heavy equipment case and leaned against it, at the ready to dash behind. I needed to wait until the zoom camera was just above the heads of the cast before I pushed the start button on the remote.

"Ready!"

I held Darryl in one arm, my other hand in my coat pocket around the paperback-size remote control, my thumb on the button.

"Action!"

The sixth take began, smooth and uninterrupted. The tower camera glided downward. I looked away just once to confirm Pauline Place was exposed. Her beautiful eyes were concentrating and admiring her granddaughter. That confirmed, I stepped around the big case.

Once the explosion went off, I planned to make my way through the chaos and grab the memory packs off the camera-monitoring workstation. That was a half-minute away.

As the scene played out, I lowered and pressed my shoulder against the tall case. Keeping my eyes open, I pushed the button.

"Cut!" Dice shouted.

I stared at the remote and pushed the button again.

Touch called out to the crews and cast, ordering them back to their places.

My knees gave and I fell onto my rear. My face was flush. I felt red heat and hot sweat pumping through my skin.

A couple of production assistants were eyeing me, looking puzzled and concerned as I wiped perspiration from my temple and lips. One of them handed me a bottle of water and asked, "Are you having a medical thing?"

I drank and ignored the question. Finishing the bottle, I found my feet but couldn't find any way to look around the equipment case. I could hear the next take starting, and that was enough. One of the production assistants gathered up Darryl, who I had apparently dropped, and handed him to me.

I was *stricken*, no other word applied. Making my way through the backside of the set among the equipment and support crews, I walked between the service trucks and trailers, my back to the filming under the blazing lights.

Later, in the cover of darkness, I would retrieve my failed device and figure out what part hadn't worked. But at that moment, all I was capable of was removing my clothes, parting my shower curtain, and sitting on the pan in a cold stream with Darryl in my arms.

CHAPTER 27

Film Title: Rascals – The Donner *Party*
Production Day: Thirty-Four

Frau Graves watched the girl step through the frozen brush, long rifle across her chest, some kind of pelt for a hat on her head. She entered the camp warily, scanning the wagon and dangling supply sacks. Raising her hand in a signal, she stopped a few feet from the circle of rocks around the dead fire. Scanning the camp, she walked forward cautiously.

When her hand dropped, James Reed stepped into view, followed by three other children, the last two guiding pack mules burdened with crates and sacks.

Hunkered low on the wagon, Frau Graves raised her head and caught the hunter's eyes. The long rifle swung around and aimed at her. James Reed moved to her side and tapped the rifle barrel, lowering it.

"You are?" the girl with the rifle demanded, studying Frau

Graves.

James Reed started across to the supply wagon, saying, "Frau Graves. Are the others still alive?"

Frau Graves nodded, the black veil rising and falling one time.

"Where?" James Reed scanned the camp.

Frau Graves' voice was husky with relief. "Up there." She pointed back up the mountain.

"You build a fire," he told a boy wearing a leather apron and tool belt.

"Care to the mules," he ordered the two girls working the cargo straps.

"What's their condition?" he asked Frau Graves.

"Dire. We have to hurry."

"And we will. After a meal and rest. We've been traveling nonstop."

"Rest? How long?"

"We've had a perilous climb. How many in the party up there?"

"Seven when I left."

"Only seven?"

"Starvation. Some have died."

"And… my Margret?"

"She's still with us."

"Climb down. We'll have the cook fire lit soon."

"I'll lead you to them."

"Let's talk of that later."

"We'll leave soon?"

"At first light, yes. And I'll decide who goes."

The boy in the leather apron built the fire and soon had a stew pot held over the flames, giving off the deliriously tempting scent of meat, carrots, onions, and peppers. The two mules were tied off in the grass at the edge of the camp. Frau Graves sat beside the girl with the long rifle, the others circling the fire. Wooden bowls of the stew were passed out and the meal was eaten in weary silence.

Night came, filling the sky with icy stars. With it, the winds ceased. After nodding off twice, her belly full, Frau Graves left the fire where the others were laying out their bedrolls. Climbing up onto the wagon, she nested between the boxes with her horsehair blanket.

White swirling snowflakes were falling at first light. The morning also brought a dense fog. Talking softly, James Reed moved around the fire, stirring the chosen members of his rescue party—the two mule girls.

"Morning," he whispered to each. "Let's bridle both and pack one-third of our food stores."

The girls stood, shook out and rolled up their bedding and walked to the high grass. The girl with the long rifle and the boy wearing the leather apron remained in leaden sleep.

Standing at the rear of the supply wagon, James Reed watched Frau Graves in peaceful slumber and waited a moment before gently twisting her boot heel twice. She stirred slowly but sat up quickly once she had shaken her head, clearing her mind from a dream. Looking to James Reed still holding her left boot, she pulled her blanket aside.

"We go now?" Her voice was groggy.

"I'm going now. With the mules."

"I'm ready." She scooted to the edge of the wagon.

"You're not going."

"Of course, I am."

"No, you're weakened. The other two and I are well fed and strong. You would only slow us."

Frau Graves pushed off the wagon, landing on both feet but wobbled, her head light. James Reed took her arm and steadied her.

"What I recall is a two-day climb," he said. "We'll collect everyone and bring them down."

"I'm able. I'm strong. You'll need me."

"You can barely stand, but think you can climb? It's decided. I've headed their rescue so far, so you'll remain. Restore your health. You need to be strong for the remaining descent. I'll need your help, then."

Before Frau Graves could speak, he turned his back to her and walked to the mule girls sorting through supplies. Teeth clenched, hands in fists, Frau Graves' veil trembled with anger. The worst part was he was right. When they departed, she forced herself to eat as much as she could, way beyond what she needed, determined to get strong and able as quickly as possible.

Two days later, James Reed and the girls reached the base of the cliff of iced granite. Telling them to head back and mind the mules, he went forward. Frau Graves' rope still hung down the steep rock face. After testing it, he climbed the drop line with a sack over his shoulder.

Reaching the top, he crossed through the snow, tripping on hidden rocks, but never slowing. Ten minutes later, he stopped before the silent, dismal camp, seeing the two makeshift shelters and dead fire.

"I've come to help you," he called out.

There was no reply.

Fresh snow was falling. The winds were forming waving sheets of white and the camp was graveyard still.

He went forward, watching the shelter openings for any sign of movement. Standing beside the cold fire pit, sadness nearly overcame him. He was about to turn away when movement caught his eye. At a mound of purple-stained snow, a child's back was to him, his or her elbow pumping.

"You there," he called out, relieved to see a survivor.

The child's head turned, and he recognized Sarah Graves. Under the tangles of her mangy hair, her chin and lips were stained with dried blood. She stared right through him before turning back and continuing to work the saw in her hands.

Fade to black

CHAPTER 28

Black Veil

*K*neeling before my bed soaking wet from the long shower, I wiped water from my fingers and disconnected the plastic explosive from the device. Setting the brick aside, I quickly figured out what had gone wrong. While no fault of my own, I saw how a change of the radio frequency had been the cause. Dialing to the standard setting gave me lovely red lights on both the remote and device.

After reattaching the brick to the detonator, I rewrapped my invention in its black fabric. Carrying it forward to my office, I found Darryl curled up on my chair, drenched and shivering. I went and got him a fresh dry towel. After drying him off and laying him down on the couch, I woke up my computer.

There were a number of increasingly strident and urgent

emails from studio accounting going on and on about the budget numbers. I wisely refrained from replying.

There was a message from Dice asking for funding and arrangements for a location-wrap party. By setting the date four days out, it was clear he had decided to motivate himself and the company to redouble their focus and efforts. Not privy to the script, I believed we were going to overrun the schedule, but now he wanted to meet it. Location-wrap parties before primary filming continued in the studio were common, a way for the primes to thank everyone, bring in local yokels, and stir up a good amount of goodwill buzz with the media.

"I have the funds, and I'll locate an appropriate size venue," I replied to him.

A PARTY WOULD BE a perfect place for an explosion. I decided I would personally visit and choose a fine Ann Arbor restaurant to buy off for the night. Before cocktails, dinner, and gratuitous sucking up, the entire cast and crew and locals would have a red-carpet photo op in the foyer. Marketing would provide the branded back screen and décor with my prescribed touches. Everyone of importance would, of course, attend, first stop being the bright lights and cameras in the entrance. I envisioned the A-listers acting all buddy-chummy for the press as they entered, having no idea they would be leaving in black canvas bags.

My brain elevated and hovered as creative juices swirled. I sent a message to marketing telling them the event needed an oversized mockup of a black veil for the attendees to stand beside during their grinning, bug-eyed photo op. I then sent a message to Bear telling him to have three cameras and crews in place to capture the evening for the behind-the-scenes documentary. Three cameras, three memory packs—an easy fifty million.

Looking down at my naked body, I felt my heart pounding double quick. Waves of perspiration were pumping from my skin. Four days. Then I would stroll away forever from these pretentious, wanna-be-serious filmmakers. And our stars, that flock of clueless, backstabbing, greedy lemmings with their delusions of relevancy, all of them would be deep in their nonsense right up to the moment they were extinguished by thousands of tiny holes. All I needed to do was push a button, dig through the carnage for the footage, and step into the history books. From a safe distance, of course.

Pausing the reverie, I pulled up the Denison yacht brokers' website and clicked on the listing I had saved the day before. With a few mouse clicks and some typing, I made the deposit on the eighty-foot yacht Darryl and I would sail away on, flush with money while the world panted and stroked itself over the disaster.

I was as hard as a Japanese dock worker and it was uncomfortable to stand, but I did so, heading off for a second shower with Darryl and a handful of bathing gel, then clothing and a loaner Land Rover.

Two hours later, with marketing on the phone, I left the third restaurant, the famous Café Felix on Main Street in Ann Arbor, the place booked and prepaid. I ended the call by having them repeat my requests for the foyer and restaurant decorations, all 'black veil' themed. Wheeling the Rover from downtown and entering the university streets, the sidewalks were crowded with students and residents walking and talking into their cell phones. I imagined what would be filling their screens, nailing down their fleeting attention on Friday, four days from then. Gone will be porn and breathless self-applause, replaced by the massive outburst of news about the film industry tragedy, brought to them all by, well, you know who.

Waiting at a traffic light for the stream of students to cross, I found my eyes glued to the Catholic church on the corner, recalling my youth and the forced marches into a similar house of false hope and forgiveness. A priest stood at the top of the steps talking to a grizzled old woman. "What dark secrets do you hide?" I said to the father in his long frock, not that he could hear.

The light changed and horns behind me blared as I thought about my secret within a similar black cloak. I couldn't help but smile.

Putting the Rover in gear, I sped off, taking the turns that the GPS suggested, guiding me out of the city to the country roads that led me to the film set on the backside of the ski resort.

Before heading over to the day's shooting, I sat at my desk in the RV. First things first, I booked my flight and limo for late Friday night, following the infamous wrap party at the Café Felix. Next was a call to the yacht brokerage to ensure a crew would be hired and on board and ready to raise anchor.

After the tragic and deadly explosion, I would step out of the rubble, the only survivor. Bravely facing the press, I would give them and the authorities a mournful, shocked statement about what I experienced and what I knew, which would be nada, of course.

Darryl and I would be aboard the yacht by the next day for the start of my period of mourning. Needing to be alone in my loss and grief, I would get the word out that I would return once I had bravely overcome my broken heart. A few days at sea would also allow me to monitor the press and see if any suspicion fell my way. If so, we would be twelve miles out in the safe international waters.

I planned to spend the first day out at sea kicking off the

auction for the footage. As soon as the fifty million passed through the shell and landed in my Bogotá account, I would be ready for the restoration of my director's career.

Mastering the press with my heavy-hearted courage, I would let it be known that my new mission in life was to see the rest of the movie completed. Doing so was the only way possible to honor our lost stars and help our millions of fans to overcome their loss. The aura of the tragedy and newfound appreciation for my brilliant auteur vision would ensure my return to the director's chair.

Down the road, there would be a premiere featuring my rise from the tragic ashes to guide the film through to its wonderful and healing denouement. It goes without saying that the film would ring in untold millions, reestablishing my deserved directorship of future movies.

CHAPTER 29

Film Title: Rascals – The Donner *Party*
Production Day: Thirty-Five

*J*ames Reed returned to the lower camp, followed by the two mules whose tails were being held by those who could walk, two of the three survivors from the high camp. The mule girls walked alongside the animals, encouraging them on with soft words and kind branch swings. One mule was burdened with supplies, and the second carried Francis Donner, too weak to walk, riding with her shoulders and head hung low and forward.

Frau Graves spotted them first, standing at the back of the supply wagon with knife in hand. Dropping to the ground, she ran to her sister on unsteady legs. The hunter girl with the long rifle strapped to her shoulder also saw. She was crossing the camp with her arms full of firewood. Dropping the limbs and branches, she studied the faces of the survivors of the high camp. Sarah Graves looked bewildered and confused. Margret Reed looked even worse, a madness in her eyes, her teeth chewing the inside of her cheek.

"Put on a meal," James Reed called out. "We've got bellies to fill."

No snow was falling, but the low camp had a carpet of white. Barren stalks of gray grass pushed up through the low drifts. The mule girls helped Francis Donner down before leading the mules across to the wagon to unpack them. While James Reed, Sarah Graves, and Margret Reed entered the camp on shaky footing, Francis Donner remained at the edge of the camp. She had taken to chewing on her coat sleeve, taking furtive glances at the others. Like the other children, her nose and fingers were ruined with frostbite.

Frau Graves took Sarah Graves into her arms and led her to the fire. James and Margret Reed joined them while Francis Donner raised her chin high and babbled, her eyes to the white sky above.

The hunter girl stood from the fire where meat was hanging over a branch. She went to Francis Donner, took her hand, and guided her slowly into camp.

"She's gone mad," Sarah Graves whispered.

"Where are the others?" Frau Graves held her lifelong friend close.

"Kesenberg is alive. Refused. Broken spirit and too weakened."

"And?"

"The others perished."

They turned away as the hunter girl and Francis Donner sat down before the fire. Frau Graves added a few twigs as the others put their hands out for warmth.

"Good Lord, no," the hunter girl cried out.

The others turned and saw the horror in her eyes.

Francis Donner had a seed sack open at her knees.

"This is my friend..." she explained, lifting out a heart with hanging strings of tissue, all of it covered in dried blood.

Frau Graves leaned across and placed her hand on her shoulder, trying to find her eyes in the fall of filthy, matted hair.

"Let me put her in the snow. She'll keep well."

Francis tightened her hand around the heart, her other dragging the sack up into her lap.

"Never mind. Warm yourself from the fire," the hunter girl said.

James Reed stood and stared down at the three high-camp survivors, his jaw clenched, his eyes narrowed with revulsion. Speaking to Sarah Graves and Francis Donner, he refused to look at Margret Reed, who was studying his expression.

"I'll never accept... the outrage. The offense to God."

He left the circle, Margret Reed letting out a whelp of agony.

She turned and watched him kick through the snow to the pine trees.

"Forgive me, please," she called after him. If he heard, there was no reply. He didn't return until nightfall.

The next morning, Frau Graves and the hunter girl put on snowshoes and left the camp. An hour later, the others heard the crack of the rifle.

"Relax, she's a good shot," James Reed told everyone around the fire. "I just hope she dropped something big."

On the steep side of the snow-covered hill between two gray rock faces, the hunter girl killed the mountain goat with a precise fifty-yard chest shot. After slogging through the deep snow, she and Frau Graves knelt beside the fallen animal. Both went to work fast, sharing the knife Frau

Graves had brought along, carving the fur away and slicing chunks of warm meat.

When they had filled two grain sacks, Frau Graves asked for a turn with the rifle. An hour later, she spotted a jackrabbit sixty yards off and knocked it down with a single headshot.

"Good Lord." The hunter girl admired, "You're a crack."

"I wonder what a bunny tastes like?" Frau Graves handed the rifle back and started across to retrieve it.

Back in camp, the two girls pressed most of the goat meat into the snow behind the fire. The hunter girl dumped the rest of the meat in the cooking pot over the fire. While it burned and sizzled, Frau Graves cleaned and gutted the rabbit, the others watching on. She welded the knife with precision, slicing off the fur so that it remained in one piece. No one said a word. Thirty minutes later, bowls of goat and rabbit meat were handed out.

After everyone had eaten themselves full, James Reed addressed them, his eyes avoiding theirs.

"We head out in the morning."

The other children looked across the fire to him, their faces warmed by the waving firelight. He hadn't spoken to anyone since the day before. Sarah Graves had attempted to talk to him earlier, to gain his understanding. Her efforts were met with stony silence.

Putting her arm around her sister, she spoke to all, "James is right, we have to get down off this mountain as best we can. Tomorrow and the following days will be dangerous."

Unbuttoning her coat, she held it open, revealing the papers inside the lining pocket. "I've signed a land grant of six-hundred acres to each of you to add iron to your stride. I hope it adds promise to your hearts."

Weary eyes rose around the fire.

"These used to belong to Hastings," she continued. "Not anymore."

"And my people? Uncle George and Tamzene back at the Alder camp," Francis Donner asked. "Certainly, they deserve a share. And rescue."

"Once we reach a settlement, we'll send a new team for them. I'll see to it that everyone who makes it off this cursed mountain will receive a grant of good land."

Francis Donner lowered her eyes, slowly shaking her head. "Pray with me." She put her disfigured hands together.

Three of the children raised their hands as she began the Our Father, the others looking on.

Frau Graves climbed to her feet and trudged to the second tent, carrying the rabbit pelt.

"I've got a new pillow. Pray all night if you like." She climbed in under the canvas.

The following morning, the mule girls attempted to bridle the mules to the supply wagon without success, so the party headed out on foot. Each of them carried or shouldered a sack of supplies or meat. The hunter girl led the way with Frau Graves at her side, followed by James and Margret Reed. Francis Donner was astride a mule, still too weak to walk. Sarah Graves brought up the rear, expecting some to fall and ready to help them on.

A mile out, they faced heavy drifts across the face of the mountain. The steep and treacherous rock face towered over them. Far in the distance below were more mountains, most barren of trees. The winds rose, sending up blinding waves of white and stinging cold.

They descended in a ragged line, the snow often overhead.

By late afternoon, they entered a steep and treacherous crevasse of massive rocks, ice cracking underfoot. From there on until nightfall, they snaked, climbed, and struggled downward.

Time and again, Sarah Graves stepped around sacks dropped into the snow. Shouldering one that held meat, she abandoned the others, except for one that held their firebox, hand saw, and knife.

Fade to black

CHAPTER 30

The Wrap

*A*rriving at Café Felix two hours before the flashbulb festivities, I stood off to the side while the finishing touches were made to the foyer décor. The film's title, Rascals – The Donner *Party*, was printed on a ten by twelve-foot backdrop where the cast and crew would have their photographs taken. I had my hand in the design, insisting that the 'Y' at the end of Party have a falling drop of blood. Beside the poster stood the oversized black top hat and veil to be included in all photographs taken. A nice touch, I had to say. It was also one of my creative strokes.

There were gold Xs of gaffing tape on the crimson carpet marking where to stand. The Xs

also ensured that the faces of the stars, primes, crews, and guests would be captured with their final smiles and grins. In addition to the two movie cameras from the set, the documentary crew I hired was bustling and chatting around their equipment.

I crossed to the black veil display and casually looked it over. Stepping around behind it, I looked around before secreting the device inside its hollow back.

"Flor, can you stand on the marks for a test?" the documentary director called to me.

"Gladly," I agreed and took off my heavy winter coat. Setting it aside, I strolled to the center X.

I had plenty of time before I took to hiding out in the kitchen with the remote in my hands.

Some called out "Striking" from behind a camera. My forward view was obliterated by hot, brilliant light from the three 300-AARIs.

"Audio rolling," carried from behind the wall of white.

And there I was in the rarified air and elevated status of center stage, proud and solid with a significant presence.

"Cameras speeding," the camera operator said.

Sensing the extended boom mic overhead, I put my hands on my hips and gave the best side of my face to the audience, narrowing one eye in an exacting and knowing intelligent gaze.

"Flor, mic test, please."

I needed a line, and no words came. I was lost in the experience and pose with no writer, no script. My brain flicked through tattered bits of famous quotes and dialogue. Getting only fragments, my hands clenched, and I felt perspiration beading across my upper lip.

"Flor. Anything."

Topics and memories scrolled forward and dissolved. Wiping my lips with my suit sleeve, it finally came to me. Share a fine and intelligent comment on my last directorship. I cleared my throat and returned my sweaty hand to my hip.

I decided to start with, "When I directed the well-respected..."

Two hands began clapping, interrupting and distracting me. I looked away from the cameras to see who it was. The clapping was loud and slow, like that given out of false courtesy rather than respect and appreciation.

A skinny man stood further back in the restaurant, half in and half out of an alcove. His clothing was in shambles and his face was distantly familiar. I scrolled through memories trying to place him. He was twenty feet away, his eyes were hidden by a dirty baseball hat. He had my coat over his arm.

"Flor?" the director called from behind the cameras and lights.

Ignoring him, I watched the man continuing to clap his hands. His scrawny chin raised and I saw his full face and recognized the skeletal Roy Three from the wrecking yard and barn. His thin and wasted face stretched into a smile of bad teeth.

I took an involuntary step backward off the X, my thoughts spinning and confused.

He raised his bony hand and offered me a strange and baffling dainty finger wave goodbye. His other hand went inside my coat pocket.

"What are you doing here?" I demanded. "Someone, get him out of here."

No one moved forward. When Roy Three raised the remote control overhead, there were shouts and the front door of the restaurant crashed open, followed by running feet.

"No!" I screamed.

Stepping back into the alcove, Roy Three pressed his finger on the trigger button

CHAPTER 31

Film Title: Rascals – The Donner *Party*
Production Day: Thirty-Six

The staggering, starving children were three days into their descent when they came to the last mark on a rock left by James Reed during his climb to them. In the freezing shadow of a towering rock, they stood in a circle, staring blankly at the next challenge. The marker was encouraging, but before them were wind-torn pine and spruce trees at the edge of yet another deep and treacherous gorge.

"We pause here," Sarah Graves ordered. "Rest for a few minutes."

She stood with the mule girls talking about the safest way to start the next descent. Rain started to fall through the dense fog, the sun overhead a round ghost of itself. Within minutes, the party was drenched and chilled to the bone.

Sarah Graves called for them to press on before the stream far below became a torrent.

The two mule girls took the lead after helping Francis Donner down onto her unsteady feet. Guiding the mules down through the boulders, the two girls encouraged the mules on with tugs and tongue clicks. Weaving down through the rocks, the others struggled, grasping the slick stones and hanging branches. Their line stretched out, James Reed doing his best to encourage Francis Donner to continue.

"Come now, one foot after the other," he prodded her when she faltered on the slick rocks through the icy rain.

Once again, Sarah Graves brought up the rear, ready to help anyone who might hesitate or stop.

The weary and starving children climbed downhill at a slow and cautious pace. A third of the way along, what had been a stream beside them was a wild overrun river. The clouds of rising mist and the splashing water made each handhold difficult to spot and grasp. Frau Graves was the only not to slow down, moving out ahead of the two girls and mules. When not looking for where to take her next step, her veiled eyes were to the west, searching for the promised California.

The party reached the bottom of the gorge and dropped from where they stood in a field of rocks. After talking with Sarah Graves, James Reed took the lead, encouraging everyone back up on their feet. With his arm around Francis Donner, holding her steady, they started out again.

Some hours later, the rains ended as they entered a dense strand of oaks and maples. Beams of warm sunlight came down through the trees, giving slight relief to chilled skin and sodden clothing.

A mile farther, they stood on the top of a hill of oak trees. The sound of rushing water carried to them, the new stream or river unseen. While the others stood and listened, Frau Graves headed out. A few minutes later, they followed.

At the base of the hill, a river of fast waters stood between them and the tree-lined bank on the other side. Frau Graves entered the frigid waters first, arms out to her side for balance. Halfway across, the racing water was up to her chin and trying to sweep her away. Fighting for footholds on the slippery rocks, she pressed on. As the others watched, she climbed out on the other side and entered the shadow of the trees.

One by one, the others followed. The mules were led across first, followed by James Reed leading Francis Donner by the hand. When everyone was across, they fell to the rocks and carpet of golden pine needles.

"A fire, please," Margret Reed begged Sarah Graves. "We're soaked and freezing."

"I would if we had any matches left," she replied. "We need to press on."

Moving deeper inside the thickening of pine trees, their footsteps were made easier as mud and weed replaced the rocks.

James Reed joined Frau Graves at the lead. A mile along, they came upon a trail marked by wagon wheel ruts and hoof prints. Standing on the top of the hill, before them was a meadow of waving wet grasses. Taking to the trail, they let it lead the way down and across the field. As they crossed, sunlight sneaked down through the clouds, forming warm pools to linger in, if only for a moment.

A mile or so farther, the children climbed another hill of rocks and brush. Reaching the top, James Reed stopped. Frau Graves did as well, taking in the next obstacle. The rest of the party spread out to their sides, forming a ragged line. Above their heads, the last of the clouds rolled eastward and they were warmed by sunlight coming from the bold blue sky.

A quarter-mile off, a wide river ran dangerous and fast. Beyond its banks was an endless field of spring grass.

Frau Graves started out first, not looking back. The other children followed slowly, weakly.

Reaching the edge of the river, Frau Graves stopped, looking into the water, searching the rocks for handholds.

"We'll cross to the south." James Reed stepped up beside her, pointing to a widening of the river, suggesting shallower waters. Frau Graves nodded in agreement and moved out along the riverbank with the others following.

Being the tallest, James Reed tied a rope around his waist and entered the waters first. A few yards out, the current was upon him, determined to knock him from his feet and carry him away.

Slipping and stumbling, he went all the way under twice before climbing the opposite bank. Soaked and shaking, he dragged himself up through the rocks and tied the rope to the nearest tree trunk. Turning around, he beckoned the others to follow.

"The mules go next," Sarah Graves told the two girls holding their tethers. "Margret, take one of their tails."

Margret Reed did as told while the mule girls led the animals down to the water, Francis Donner riding on the first, slumped forward and silent. The lead mule entered the river and plodded slowly, testing its bottom with hesitant hoof plants.

Frau Graves and the hunter girl watched the crossing, Sarah Graves a few yards away. She was studying the land beyond the river. A half-mile farther, smoke twisted leisurely from a chimney above a ranch house. She crossed to the other two, saying, "We go as soon as they're safely across."

The three of them stood side by side, golden sunset light flickering off the running river, warming their faces.

A group of four were coming along a foot trail from the

ranch house—three boys and a tall woman in sure, commanding strides.

Frau Graves took the hunter girl by the arm and led her into the water. The two slogged and faltered out a couple of feet into the icy water and stopped. Both saw long-lost Stanton running along the shore, shouting and waving them off.

On the opposite bank, Hastings stood, looking across the river, ignoring the mules and the others, her eyes on Sarah Graves. She wore a long coat of white-wolf fur. Pulling the hood back from her vibrant red hair, she yelled across the river.

"We've done it! The cutoff is a success!"

"A success?" Sarah Graves yelled back, "There's a trail of bodies along your alleged shortcut."

Hastings ignored that, standing at the water's edge with her three boys. Her arms were crossed, her confident chin raised, her beautiful eyes calculating. Finding a proud smile, she offered it.

Without a word, Frau Graves eased the long rifle from the hunter girl's shoulder. Knowing it was loaded and primed, she didn't bother to check as she extended the barrel.

"No!" Sarah Graves screamed, running for her, stumbling across the rocks.

On the opposite back, the three boys were frantically drawing their pistols.

Frau Graves aimed and pulled the trigger.

Across the sparkling river, Hastings was struck in the chest. The bullet tore a bloody hole in her white fur coat. She was launched backward off her feet, landing hard on the rocks and weeds. The boys about her lowered their weapons and stared. Seconds later, they started a fast retreat for the ranch houses.

Frau Graves kept the rifle raised, aimed on Hastings, ready to fire again if she moved. She continued looking down the long barrel, her finger scratching the trigger.

Hastings lay perfectly still, her legs inelegantly splayed, the rocks at her sides forming the channels for her flowing blood.

Seeing no sign of life, Frau Graves handed the rifle back to the hunter girl. Her veiled eyes steady across the water, she spoke in a tight voice, "That done, we've reached it."

"Reached what?" Sarah Graves knelt at her side, eyes wide with fright and confusion. She put her hand out to touch her sister's shoulder, to pull her close. Seeing her expression, she pulled back.

From inside the black veil, a frightening and satisfied grin showed.

Frau Graves' next words were light with childish innocence.

"The end."

ACKNOWLEDGMENTS

David Adamczyk, Assistant Director

Peter Putman, Director of Photography

Kate Shepard, Wardrobe and Makeup

Alyse Paquin, Script Supervision and Continuity

Megan Mockensturm, actress

Kara Joy Reed, actress

Brent Glover, actor

Mike T. Tremblay, actor

Dave Durham, actor

All the crew and cast of Memoirs of Wroth City and everyone at Broken Television Entertainment

Stella Wiard, another wonderful six-year-old wild-child

"Desperate Passage: The Donner Party's Perilous Journey West" by Ethan Rarick

"The Indifferent Stars Above: The Harrowing Saga of the Donner Party" by Daniel James Brown

"Go, Dog. Go!" by P.D. Eastman

"Cinematic Storytelling" by Jennifer Van Sijll

"The Five C's of Cinematography" by Joseph V. Mascelli

"Day of the Locusts," Nathaniel West's brilliant and beautiful romp through Hollywood

ABOUT THE AUTHOR

Greg Jolley earned a Master of Arts in Writing from the University of San Francisco and lives in the very small town of Ormond Beach, Florida. When not writing, he researches historical crime, primarily those of the 1800s. Or goes surfing.

ALSO BY GREG JOLLEY

Distractions

Danser

Dot to Dot

The Amazing Kazu

Murder in a Very Small Town

Where's Karen?

Malice in a Very Small Town

The Girl in the Hotel (by Gregory French)

View Finder

www.TheDansers.com

Lightning Source UK Ltd.
Milton Keynes UK
UKHW020231030720
365951UK00009B/399/J

9 781087 885469